the
thousand
natural
shocks

the thousand natural shocks

Michael Sáenz

illustrations by Alex Fox

Tim Palin Creative Pages · Brooklyn, New York
www.timpalincreative.com

The Thousand Natural Shocks is a work of fiction.
Characters, locations and events are all from the imagination of the author.

Copyright © 2011 by Michael Ignacio López

Book design: Tim Palin Creative
Illustrations: Alex Fox

ISBN-13: 978-1482577402
ISBN-10: 1482577402

Printed in U.S.A

www.thethousandnaturalshocks.com

info@thethousandnaturalshocks.com

Twitter: @CharlesSiskin

www.facebook.com/TheThousandNaturalShocks

www.facebook.com/michael.lopezsaenz

For my Mother, who made it easy.
For my Sister, who listened without judgment.
For my Brother, who stood up for me.

contents

a word from the author

I think it's important to say a word or two about why I wrote this book. And who the book is for. Many people will look at it and think that it fits in a specific category . . . or that it doesn't fit into any. And I guess they would all be right.

This book is not necessarily just for teenagers, although it is about a teenager and takes place during his early high school years. By the same token, it is not intended just for adults, although the time period will bring back many fond memories for those of the older set. This book is not just for gay or questioning teens, or just for teens who self-identify as straight, either.

The themes are mature, but there is nothing gratuitous or salacious in it.

I wrote this story as a story for almost anyone.

I intended it to be read by parents and their children, by people of any sexual orientation and by anyone who has been bullied or who has bullied or who remembers what a terrible and wonderful time high school can be. I would like this to be a story that will start a conversation, or maybe a whole lot of conversations, among people who may believe that they have nothing in common. And maybe after these conversations, the reader might find her or himself a little closer to someone they previously thought was completely foreign to her or him.

Most of all, I would like this to be a story that offers hope.

–Michael Sáenz

this is the introduction

This is the introduction to my story. I have been told that introductions should be short, snappy and to the point. It kind of doesn't really matter to me, because I usually skip the introduction when I'm reading a book, and I'm not really sure why a book needs an introduction when I think it's better to just get right to the story. I guess it makes the story seem classy or important so I'll give it a shot.

My name is Charles Siskin. Nobody calls me Charlie or Chuck or Chuckles or Big C or anything like that. Everyone just calls me Charles. That's about the only bit of real logistical information that you're going to get.

There are a lot of things that I won't explain in this story. Or maybe I should say that there are a lot of things that I won't explain in this *narrative*[1]. My creative writing teacher, Brother Marvin, says I should practice using my vocabulary and saying exactly what I mean. But I also know that looking up a bunch of words in the dictionary can be a pain in the ass. So I have included, for your convenience, a handy set of footnotes on all of the new words I learned my freshman year. The definitions are official and correct and actually taken from the dictionary, but that seemed a little dry, so I've included my own little additions.

---

[1] **nar•ra•tive** [**nar**-*uh*-tiv] *n.* 1. a telling of events, either true or fictional; a story 2. a work of literature or a book that contains the representation of an event or story 3. the practice, technique or art of narrating

Here's a perfect example: *This book is a narrative.*

You know, I think it's kind of funny how knowing and using a lot of words can be really great in some places and can get you into a shitload of trouble in others. Like in class. Teachers really pant and wheeze and get all excited when you use a lot of big words. On the other hand, if you use those same words in regular conversation with friends or students or other ordinary people, they think you're a snob or a teacher's pet or a wuss and sometimes that leads to getting the crap kicked out of you.

Which bring me to an important point: I'll be leaving a lot of details out of this narrative. They won't be the kind of details that someone reading this absolutely has to know. But I won't tell you what city I'm in or what the real name of the school is and all of the names (except for mine) will be changed to protect the innocent (and the guilty).

But these kinds of details aren't that important. The important things, like the events, are real.

Just imagine that this story is happening in any city in America . . . maybe any city in the world. I have to believe that my story is not so uncommon. Even though I might feel like I'm the only weirdo like me in the whole universe, that can't be true. There must be boys like me all over the place. There must be. I have to believe that. If I don't believe it, then what's the point?

So ends the introduction. As a start, I would say that this introduction has really classed the hell out of the story so far. What do you think?

PART I

the undiscover'd country

presenting: chapter one

I'm going to do my best to keep this story organized. I have a tendency to ramble. So with this in mind, I will start at the beginning of my life and give you a little background information about me, so that you can understand me better as a character and *empathize*[2] with me and some of the effed up things that happened to me and the even more effed up things I did in response to the effed up things that happened to me.

Brother Marvin would be so proud. Maybe I should cool it on the use of terms like "effed up." Well, at least he would approve of my attempts to organize my thoughts and the events into some semblance of order. Here's the order I choose: *chronological*[3].

So, Chapter One begins with my childhood.

I was pretty happy as a child, but then again I didn't know any better.

---

[2]**em•pa•thize** [em-puh-thayz] *v.* to experience empathy: *his account of the events allowed me to empathize with his experience*

I don't understand why they are always telling you that you can't define a word by using the word in the definition, and then you look in the dictionary and they do exactly that. So to clarify, empathy is the ability to identify with or imagine what it's like to feel the feelings or think the thoughts of another person.

[3]**chron•o•log•i•cal** [kron-*uh*-**loj**-i-k*uh*l] *adj.* 1. arranged in or according to the order of time: he told the events in chronological order. 2. relating to chronology: *chronological age*

I'm not sure that I really succeeded in putting the events of this story in the order that they happened. Looking back over it, I think I may have jumped around a little. But you get the gist.

You should probably know that I am an only child. Thank God for small favors. When I was very young (three or so) I was really cute (if you can believe the pictures) and my mom used to dress me in natty little outfits like shorts and crisp white shirts and bow ties and the occasional blazer. If you go by the pictures, it looked like I was always ready to step onto a yacht or attend a summer party thrown by the Great Gatsby. My hair was always combed and slicked down and I never had any bruises or scrapes on my knees.

I don't remember a lot from my childhood. I think I have a tendency to forget everything as soon as it happens (which makes for a really good reason to write this book—so I don't forget it all before I hit my sophomore year). But there are a couple of *salient*[4] (go, Brother Marvin!) points that I do remember and that will provide you, the reader, with great insight into who I am.

Let's start with elementary school. I love my parents, but they probably didn't do me any favors by starting me out in school a year early. My birthday was in November, which was right on the cutoff date or something. My mom says it was because I was really verbal and very clearly ahead of other four-year-olds. By the time I hit kindergarten I already knew my alphabet and could read Dick and Jane. They even had me see a shrink to see if I could handle the stress of being younger than everybody else. Apparently, I could.

And, even more unusual, when I was in the first grade I was in love with most of the boys in my class.

Now it may be at this point that I lose a good number of readers. "We didn't know it was going to be one of those kinds of books," you may be thinking. "We like stories about *normal* people doing *normal* things like a boy playing with trucks and coming of age and falling in love with a girl who is slightly out of his league but his winning personality causes her to reevaluate her previous standards and she breaks up with her

---

[4]**sa•li•ent** [**sey**-lee-*uh*nt, **seyl**-*yuh*nt] *adj.* 1. that which moves by leaps or springs: *jumping* 2. jetting or projecting upward: *a salient spring of water* 3. an outstanding or pertinent feature 4. prominent or standing out; of notable significance

I always get this word confused with saline, like the saline solution we used in Biology class.

football-player boyfriend in a juicy scene that takes place in the cafeteria and she sees that there is so much more to a person than just muscles and she and the hero go to the prom together and dance to a song by Spandau Ballet."

I feel really bad that I am disappointing you so early in the story, but this is not that kind of book. Maybe I should have mentioned this in the introduction . . . so much for great organization. Somewhere Brother Marvin is clucking his tongue and shaking his head. If it's any consolation, I was in love with most of the girls, too. But in an entirely different way.

Now. You might ask yourself, "How can a first grader know that he is in love with anyone?" But I assure you that it was true. Despite my *deviant*[5] tendencies I was a very loving little boy. Just ask my mother. There were times when I was so loving that she would have to encourage me to go outside and play or go watch TV or something because I was driving her crazy with my clinginess and need for hugs and attention.

So anyway, back to the boys. I remember being in love with most of the boys in my class at Woodvale Elementary. It was kind of like they were another species. They were rough and strong and didn't seem to mind getting dirty and I really wanted to kiss a good number of them. I'm pretty sure I was as foreign to them as they were to me, and they mostly avoided me or called me names.

The only exception was a boy named Billy Burlington who at the time seemed like he was six feet four. He was taller than the other boys and I guess he was pretty dumb because he

---

[5]**de•vi•ant** [**dee**-vee-*uh*nt] *adj.* 1. straying from the accepted norm, especially in regards to behavior. *n.* 2. that which deviates from the norm.

You know. Like a pervert.

didn't have the sense to avoid me the way they did. Or maybe it was just because he sat next to me and he felt like he had to talk to me. Once when we were in the bathroom he showed me his wiener . . . very casual and offhand, like it was a marble he carried around in his pocket or something. Oddly enough, he was one of the few boys in the class that I didn't want to kiss, but we were very good friends.

So, as I said, the boys tended to avoid me—which was okay by me because I preferred to hang out with the girls. I liked the games they played, I liked the stuff they talked about, and they were fun. And for the most part they weren't mean to me like the boys could be. They didn't push me down or tell me to "beat it" or call me names like crybaby or cream puff. And the girls were pretty. They combed their hair and kept their clothes neat like I did and were just generally less foreign than the boys.

Even though I don't remember a whole lot about this time (as I previously stated), I do remember one incident that makes me cringe when I look back on it now. One day our teacher, Mrs. Horseford (we all called her Mrs. Horseface behind her back) was absent and we had a substitute. Unlike Mrs. Horseface, the sub was young and pretty and didn't give us prunes as an afternoon snack. At any rate, she was young and pretty and cool. And as usually happens when there is a sub, we didn't do a lot of work that day. At one point, right after recess, she asked the class if anyone wanted to have a talent show. Of course, we did. This was when I decided it was time to make my theatrical debut. With four of my best little girlfriends, I decided we would perform our version of "Spoon Full of Sugar" from the movie Mary Poppins.

I know, I know.

But I had the record at home. I listened to it all the time

and it was one of my favorite movies. So we went out into the hall, practiced it and then came in and performed it for the class. The only thing that saves this story from being entirely horrifying is that when the rest of the class (especially the boys) stared at us, slack-jawed in disbelief as we sang and danced, this awesome sub (I can't for the life of me remember her name) saved us from utter humiliation by joining in on the last chorus. And I loved her for that.

Needless to say, with events like these popping up all over my childhood, I spent a good deal of my time becoming more and more isolated from the norm. To make things worse, I was so ahead of everybody else that my parents thought it would be a good idea if I skipped a grade. I guess I seemed like I was bored, which made me disrupt the class a lot with my constant fidgeting and insistence on talking non-stop to anyone within earshot. So after elementary school, up a grade I went.

Also, I was an odd, effeminate little boy, and the older I got the stranger my classmates thought I was. By the time I moved on to John Glenn Middle School, I was pretty much (get ready for this one, Brother Marvin) a *pariah*[6], and spent most of my time alone. My weird personality (namely a fussy way of dressing, a clearly feminine way of walking and talking, a dislike of sports or other typically boy-type pastimes), which could be put down as just a little odd when I was in elementary school, couldn't be so easily ignored in middle school. In middle school everything is about being normal, especially when it comes to how boys should act and how girls should act.

---

[6]**pa•ri•ah** [p*uh*-**rahy**-*uh*] *n.* 1. a member of the low caste in southern India 2. a person who is outcast or avoided: an outcast

I always thought this word would make a dandy first name . . . if it didn't mean what it meant, I mean.

Seventh grade was the first time I got called gay—and queer and fag. By the time I reached eighth grade it was pretty bad. I don't think I had a single friend, and just the thought of going to school each day was misery. Which really sucked, because I genuinely liked school—classes, I mean. I enjoyed learning and ended up spending most of my time talking to my teachers and wishing I was an adult.

I gradually began to realize that I didn't understand kids my age. They seemed to speak a different language from me, and they were interested in all kinds of strange things. Even the girls, who up until middle school had been my friends, started to change.

All the boys seemed to want to do was fight or play sports or make stupid jokes about dicks. And the girls suddenly became obsessed with gossiping and fixing their hair and going to dances.

I spent most of my time reading. On any given day you could find me walking around the halls with a copy of Alex Haley's *Roots* or Margaret Mitchell's *Gone with the Wind* tucked under my arm. And I stood apart from everyone, watching these alien children as they crowded the halls and spoke to each other about things that I thought were stupid or unimportant. I wondered how the hell I got to this place called middle school and what I was doing here. Was I sent from another galaxy to study an alien life form, a primitive culture on an unexplored planet? It seemed so unfair.

Even though I was pretty miserable, I somehow never seemed to put the blame for my situation on myself. I never asked myself "what's wrong with me?" but instead asked myself "what's wrong with everyone else?"

It's true that there were a couple of moments when I sat

outside on the bleachers overlooking the sports fields wallowing in self pity and thinking it might be easier if I just killed myself. But I couldn't imagine how I would do it. And besides, why should I kill myself when there was nothing wrong with me and everyone else was an asshole? That really seemed unfair.

But the prospect of enduring four years in high school seemed unbearable. The public high school that I was set to attend was called James Madison High School. It was located about a ten minute drive away from John Glenn. And I felt pretty sure that it was just going to be a bigger, more intense version of the middle school hell I was in now.

In spite of whatever strength I had developed to stand up to the daily tortures and humiliations of middle school, I didn't think I was going to survive four more years of the same (and worse) at James Madison. So what could I do?

ladies and gentlemen: chapter two

One of the nicest things you can say about my parents is that they leave me alone. I don't mean they neglect me. They just respect that I like to be on my own. Okay, that's not exactly true. My dad (Peter) leaves me alone because he doesn't understand me (any more than I understand him). I think for him it's a lot like I am a foreign exchange student who lives in his house. He's nice to me. He says good morning and drives me places, like he used to drive me to dance class twice a week. But we have a rather formal acquaintanceship.

My mother (Adriana) has always gotten me. After I left the clingy stage of childhood, I think she just totally understood my need for privacy.

When you are an only child, the relationship you have with your parents is much more like being equals—at least it was for me. When my parents had friends over, it was completely normal for me to sit with all of them in the living room, sipping a beverage and listening to the conversation. Even as far back as age six or seven. These were some people who made sense to me. They talked about interesting things and told great stories and fascinating jokes. I suppose it's just one more thing that makes me totally uncool to kids my own age: I don't hate my parents or adults in general.

One of my favorite adults is my mother's friend Sammy (short for Samantha) Della Franca. Sammy is very cool and talks to me like she would any other adult. She wears big, chunky jewelry and smells like Chanel No. 5 and Pall Malls.

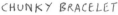

CHUNKY BRACELET   CHANEL N°5   PALL MALLS

One night during the fall of my eighth grade year, Sammy came over to visit. My mother and Sammy sat in the living room drinking glasses of cabernet and smoking and talking about people they knew. I sat with them, drinking Dr. Pepper out of a wine glass.

"So then I asked her how she knew that Trudy's husband was cheating on her," said Sammy, "and she said that she had seen them together at Pancho's Mexican Buffet, sitting in the corner and holding hands and kissing on each other like there was no tomorrow."

"You're kidding," my mother replied, so engrossed in the story it looked like her eyes were about to drop out of her skull.

"That's what she said. So then I asked her if Mario had ever cheated on her."

"No, you didn't!"

"I did. I said, 'So, Juanita, do you think Mario has ever dipped his pen in another inkwell?' " Sammy brayed out a single sharp laugh.

"Sammy, you didn't!"

"Of course I did. And she said that she knew she could trust him completely."

"How would she know that?"

"She said because he was deathly afraid of getting the clap."

"Oh, my God!" They both burst into hysterical giggles.

"Then I asked her if she had ever—"

"Sammy, you didn't."

"And do you know what she said?" Sammy choked on her laughter then took a swig of her wine. "She said: 'I would never cheat on Mario. I'm not that type of woman. I was a virgin when I married him, and I don't know if—*they*—come in sizes.' "They both erupted in howls of laughter. Sammy spilled some wine on the coffee table and choked out an apology between brays of laughter to which my mother waved her hand in a gesture that said "don't worry about it.'"

After a couple of minutes they were able to compose themselves. Sammy lit up a fresh cigarette and sat back on the sofa, tucking her bare feet under her.

"So," Sammy said, exhaling a long stream of smoke, "what else is new? What's cracking, Egghead?" She called me Egghead because I read a lot.

"Absolutely nothing," I said. "School, school, blah, blah, blah."

"What are you talking about, blah, blah, blah?" my mother said. "It's that kind of attitude that's affecting your grades."

"Are you having problems with your grades?" said Sammy.

"No. My grades are fine."

"Your grades are average, my son. And you are anything but average."

"Of course his grades are average," said Sammy. "He's in that crap-tub of a school. He's not being challenged."

My mother and I looked at each other. Sammy tapped her ashes in the ashtray with a gesture that punctuated her typical ability to cut right to the heart of the matter.

"Do you think that's true, Charles?" my mother said.

"I don't know. I never really thought about it."

"Of course it's true!" said Sammy. The boy's a genius, aren't you, Egghead?" She winked one false-eyelashed eye at me. "What you should do is send him to that Loyola High School downtown. It's the best private school in the city."

And just like that Sammy had presented me with what I thought would be the answer to all my problems. Get the hell out of public school. Go to a private school where there are students who actually care about learning. And get away from all those jerks that made my life miserable.

Loyola was going to be the answer to all of my problems.

So I asked my parents if I could go to Loyola.

"What for?" my dad said.

"So I can get a decent education," I semi-lied.

"Well, it would be a little—inconvenient," my mother said. "How would we get you there? It's so far from the house."

"How much does this school cost?" my dad asked, his eyes narrowed to slits.

"I don't know." I said. "But I'll bet if I went there, I could get into any college in the country."

"Hm," he said.

"That's a good point," my mother said.

"Besides, if I don't get a decent education, how the hell am I going to get a great job and make millions of dollars and take care of the both of you when you can't feed or dress yourselves?"

They were both silent for a moment.

"Your father and I will talk it over."

After a couple of days they broke the good news to me. I could go to Loyola the following year. So at the tender age of thirteen, I found myself facing high school.

I did all the research myself. I signed up for the entrance exam, aced it, and just like that I was out of public school hell and off to St. Ignatius Loyola High School. As far as I was concerned, this meant that I was about to start a new life—a better life—a life that didn't consist of names and ridicule and being surrounded by alien dinks. St. Ignatius Loyola would be my salvation. Right?

and in this corner—
chapter three

St. Ignatius Loyola is an all-boys Catholic military high school founded by the Jesuits in 1907. The school is located on the edge of the downtown area in a building that was erected (heehee) in 1932. It has broad steps leading up to the front and an impressive *façade*[7] that looms over the boulevard that it faces. Enrollment is about eight hundred students.

---

[7]**fa•çade** [*fuh*-**sahd**] *n.* 1. in architecture, the front or face of a building, especially one given special treatment 2. a fake, shallow or superficial appearance

It suddenly strikes me as kind of interesting that I'm using this word to describe the front of the school building, when I could just as easily use it to describe how I've lived my life from one day to the next doing my best to keep up the illusion that everything is okay.

Located directly across the street is an all-girls Catholic school called St. Cecilia's, founded by an order of Dominican nuns. Later I would find out that students regularly crossed the street to attend classes at the other school. So neither school was really all boys or all girls. I had great expectations for Loyola. They were really misguided expectations, but they were great.

You see, everything I had learned about private schools I got from stuff I had read: *The Catcher in the Rye, A Separate Peace, So Much Unfairness of Things.* To say that I had romanticized what would be my experience at Loyola would be a huge understatement. In my head I had pictures of handsome boys wearing blazers and ties that bore the school colors, their hair combed neatly in a fifties' style whiffle. On the grounds surrounding the school there would be teams of fit young men playing lacrosse, and here and there would be boys sitting under trees reading books in Latin. So to be fair, Loyola didn't stand a chance when held up to this ridiculous standard.

But still, it didn't have to disappoint me so completely.

I walked into Loyola as a full-fledged student on Tuesday, September 4th, 1979 (Monday was Labor Day). Freshmen were called in a day earlier than the rest of the student body for Orientation Day. The school had wide halls, stone floors, and dark wood paneling that was polished to a high gloss and extended from the floors to halfway up the walls.

I was wearing black slacks, a starched light blue button-down shirt and a tie I had found that not so coincidentally displayed the school colors (navy and silver). The school had a dress code! No jeans, no sneakers, no shirts without collars!

I carried a brand-new leather satchel (a gift from Sammy),

the strap across my chest, filled with a trapper keeper, pens (black, blue, and red), pencils (no. 2), a ruler, a protractor, a compass, a calculator, a pocket dictionary, and my well-worn copy of William Faulkner's *The Sound and the Fury*. Clearly I was ready for anything.

TRAPPER KEEPER
PENS
RED
BLUE
BLACK
PENCIL PROTRACTOR COMPASS
SATCHEL
FAULKNER'S
THE SOUND & THE FURY
CALCULATOR

I followed my schedule to room 312, up on the third floor. This was to be my homeroom and my English class, led by someone with the last name of Holly.

I walked into a classroom unlike any I had seen before. The ceilings were at least twelve feet tall. One wall was all windows, from waist height all the way up to the ceiling, framed and silled in dark wood, worn down from years of use. There were ceiling fans, since there was no central air, and all the windows were open. Even though it was September, August hadn't quite let go and it was at least ninety degrees in the room.

The teacher's desk was directly ahead of me as I stepped through the door. Behind the desk stood a really odd-looking man. He was tall, at least six feet, and probably weighed no more than one-fifty after a good meal. His skin was pale and smooth, like the belly of a fish. He wore horn-rimmed glassed with thick lenses that made his eyes appear to bulge like two poached eggs. He had dark hair, worn short and parted on the side, but the top had a flip to it like that little elf who wants to be a dentist on the "Rudolph the Red-Nosed Reindeer" Christmas special. He wore a black suit that hung on his lanky frame like on a scarecrow's, a white shirt, and a narrow black tie. This, I discovered, was the uniform of the religious order of brothers that ran the school.

As I came through the door, he looked me up and down and then spoke, addressing me in a voice that sounded suspiciously like Kermit the Frog's. This made everything he said sound unintentionally dry and comical. I think it's really important that you get the sound of this bizarre voice, so from now on, whenever he speaks I'm going to use italics.

"Come in, come in."

I blurted out a laugh, sure that the voice must be a joke.

"Is something funny?" he said, frowning slightly.

"N-no, no. Of course not. I'm sorry." I said, stepping towards him.

"You must be——?" he asked, his eyes bulging out farther.

"Charles. Charles Siskin. Are you Mister Holly?"

"You won't find many misters on the faculty here," he said. *"Here at Loyola we are all brothers. I believe I know you, Mr. Siskin. You may call me Brother Marvin."*

"Oh, of course. I'm sorry, sir. Brother Marvin."

"*Have a seat, Charles. Third row, fourth seat back,*" he said, after briefly consulting his list and his seating chart. Here, already, was a man I could appreciate. He had a seating chart. My kind of guy. And I'm still not sure to this day, but I think he smiled to himself a little as I turned to take my seat.

As I walked up the row I noticed that there was a boy already seated directly in front of my desk. He was small and had feminine features, light hair and glasses that were about three sizes too big for his face. As I walked up the row, I caught him looking at me and he quickly looked away. I sat down at my desk.

"Hi. My name's Charles," I said to the back of the boy's head.

After a full minute he turned around toward me. He couldn't quite seem to meet my eyes. When he spoke, his voice was very high and girlish. What was it with this school and weird voices?

"Hi," he said. "I'm Thtuart."

"I beg your pardon?"

"My name is Thtuart. Thtuart Thimpthon."

The poor boy lisped.

And he had three s's in his name: Stuart Simpson.

"Hi, Th—Stuart," I said, extending my hand. Stuart placed his limp fish of a hand in mine and shook it weakly.

"*All right, gentlemen. Please take your seats.*"

The other boys in the class sat down and looked expectantly up at Brother Marvin. Brother Marvin cleared his throat and began passing out mimeographed pieces of paper.

"*Take one of each of these sheets and pass the rest back, please.*"

The handouts consisted of general school policies, a school calendar and such.

Brother Marvin had an unsettling way of not actually looking at anyone when he was speaking, almost as if he was addressing a group of people slightly to the right and above where we were all sitting.

"Theriouthly," Stuart said, turning to pass the papers back to me. "That Brother Marvin hath the weirdetht voithe I've ever heard."

I took the papers and looked at him.

Due to alphabetizing, Stuart and I not only sat one behind the other, but we were assigned lockers right next to each other. I was actually kind of relieved. While he was a bit strange, he was definitely not threatening, and he was quiet (which I liked). He didn't seem compelled to make small talk, and when homeroom was over and we were instructed to head to the gym for some kind of freshman general meeting, he very naturally walked with me, quiet and looking around at the other boys. In the gym, he sat next to me. It seemed I had made my first friend at Loyola.

As we sat in the gym, I looked around at the other boys in my new school. They seemed older than me, somehow. It was clear that a couple of the boys actually shaved. I scanned the crowd for any temptingly handsome faces. There were probably about a hundred of us in the gym, and already I had spotted a good five or six young men that were what I would consider to be good looking.

Author's Note: Now at this point it occurs to me that you might be thinking that the only real reason I had for wanting to change schools was so that I could be in an all boy environment. And I won't lie to you. The idea didn't stink. Okay, okay, if I am being totally honest, it was there, in the back of my mind, as a *perquisite*[8] of being a student at Loyola. Or maybe it was closer to the front of my mind. But in all honesty my primary reasons were, first, to get away from the Neanderthals in public school and, second, to get the best education I could. Being surrounded by cute boys was merely a perquisite.

As my eyes studied the crowd, I noticed that the buzz and chatter had begun to die down. I looked up at the stage and saw that a brother had walked to the podium and was standing looking over the crowd, willing us to quiet down with his stern face and eyes. Amazingly enough it was working. The gym suddenly fell silent and all eyes were on him.

"Good morning gentlemen. My name is Brother Baker and I am the Dean of Students here at St. Ignatius Loyola High School. On behalf of the faculty and staff, I would like to welcome you, the members of the class of 1983."

The boys erupted in applause, which seemed to irritate Brother Baker instead of please him. He waited patiently for the applause to die down, nothing even closely resembling a smile ever touching his lips.

"St. Ignatius Loyola is regarded as the best secondary school in this city. That is not pride or bragging, but fact. We possess a spotless academic record with nearly one hundred percent of our students going on to higher education. Many of you will

---

[8]**per•qui•site** [**pur**-kwuh-zit] *n.* 1. a benefit, payment or privilege incidental to regular payment, income or wages: *As a perquisite he received season tickets to the opera and had use of the company jet.* 2. gratuity, tip 3. that which is claimed as an exclusive right or possession: *The Duke considered it a perquisite to receive the best of the new spring lambs.*

Once at a McDonald's I saved a kid from choking on the toy from his happy meal. *Learning first aid in military class was an unforeseen perquisite of attending SILHS.*

proceed to the best colleges and universities in the country. As such, we have an extremely high expectation for the young men who attend this school. You have already proved yourselves remarkable by passing an extremely rigorous entrance exam. But you will find that we will ask you to prove yourselves over and over again, on a daily basis. We expect you to excel here among the best and brightest, in academics, sports, military, the arts. This is not a place to be if you are not academically minded. Should there be any of you who choose to stand out for the wrong reasons, you will find yourself in my office. We ask nothing less of you than excellence. In return, you will carry the name of St. Ignatius Loyola with you wherever you go. It is a name that will open doors for you. Make sure that you do nothing to tarnish that name. Welcome, gentlemen. I hope you have an outstanding year."

Brother Baker left the stage, miraculously to no applause.

"What an athhole," said Stuart.

After the orientation meeting, we returned to homeroom. Stuart seemed to have come out of his shell since the whole Brother Baker speech, and began talking nonstop about all kinds of things: the school, the dress code, his dog, what we might have for lunch, when the girls were going to show up, even (oddly) that he had just found out recently that raisins came from grapes, and on and on. We came back to homeroom and sat down.

"For the remainder of the day you will go to all of your classes, although the periods will be shortened because of the assembly this morning. Before you go on to your first period class, make sure that you have checked and memorized the combination to your locker. Enjoy your first day at Loyola, gentlemen. Mr. Siskin, may I see you for a moment?"

"Yes, Brother." I walked up to his desk.

"*You will see on your schedule that you have English first period. I am the teacher for that class. However, the class will not meet today. Take a study hall for period one and I will see you in homeroom and period one tomorrow.*"

"Yes, sir. But why—?"

"*I will see you tomorrow, Charles.*"

I walked out into the hall and stood for a moment, puzzled. Stuart stood at his open locker. As I walked up he tossed a single book in and slammed the locker door shut.

"Thee you later," he said as he walked down the hall. "Maybe we can thit together at lunch?" He continued down the hall without waiting for a reply.

I turned to my locker and tried the combination.

No luck.

A second time.

No luck.

I noticed the boy who had been sitting behind me come up to his locker. He had the unlikely name of Alejandro Taylor. He was at least six feet three inches tall and slim, with a narrow nose and face. He already had five o'clock shadow at ten in the morning. He opened his locker with no problem.

"Hey, listen," I said. "Do you think you could help me with this locker? I can't seem to get it open. My name is Charles, by the way."

"I don't have time to mess with you, pansy," he said, his voice dripping with contempt. "Why don't you athk your little girlfriend?" He shut his locker and stalked off down the hall.

And with that one comment, my dreams of Loyola as my salvation were crushed like a bug under someone's shoe. Whatever curse I carried had followed me here. And it had taken only a few hours for the boys in this new school to sniff me out as something odd and out of place. How could this be? How could this place be no different than the hell I had left behind? It was as if I had come into the school skipping down the halls wearing a pink tutu. Was it really so obvious? And with these questions came a horrifying thought: I had jumped out of the proverbial frying pan and into the fire. Somehow I had believed that the best place for me to be was an all-boys, Catholic, military high school. The realization of what a colossal mistake I had just made came rolling over me like a Mack truck. It was pretty clear: I was dead meat.

are you ready for . . .
chapter four?

It was like waking up on a floor covered with mousetraps. Anyplace you step will bring you potential pain—and possibly set off the rest of the mousetraps like one of those domino toppling setups. And I had no one to blame but myself.

But maybe I was blowing things all out of proportion. Just because one dolt called me a name didn't mean that everything was going in the toilet. I tried my best to keep a positive attitude. There was a lot to look forward to at this school. After all, I did have Brother Marvin as teacher for my English class. This was a good thing. Weird voice aside, Brother Marvin seemed to be pretty cool. And I would find out just how cool very quickly.

The other classes on my schedule seemed pretty typical. Algebra. Biology. American History. Of course since this was a Catholic school, Religion class was mandatory for all four years. And there was Military.

Ah, yes! Military. Maybe you thought I had forgotten to explain about the whole military thing. Apparently Ignatius of Loyola had a military background before he founded the Society of Jesus (also known as the Jesuits). The Jesuits were to be an order of educators and missionaries. It is said that the Jesuits were known for being able to go anywhere in the world in their service of the order and to live under the most extreme conditions.

At Loyola, JROTC (Junior Reserve Officer Training Corps) was required for the first two years. All freshmen and sophomores were automatically enrolled in military class and you could continue through your senior year if you chose. The school also boasted the two finest and most highly decorated high school drill teams in the state: the Saxony Rifles (Junior Varsity) and the Ignatius Company (Varsity). I had no idea what Military class would consist of, but I didn't have to wait long to find out.

I took study hall first period, then proceeded down to the basement for Military class. The room looked like a regular classroom, except that there were no windows (being in the basement and all). The boys filed in and took their seats.

After a moment, an extremely large man came into the room. He was about five feet, eight inches—wide. And about the same height. He was at least sixty years old and wore an army uniform—olive-green pants, shiny black shoes, and a khaki, short-sleeve shirt with a white t-shirt underneath. His hair was silver and cut in a severe flattop. He had a bulbous nose and wore black, plastic-rimmed glasses. And he had what appeared to be twenty to twenty-five bumps on his face and head. Were they warts? Were they boils? I didn't know. And I wasn't about to ask him.

He walked heavily to the front of the classroom, wheezing audibly as he did so. When he got to the front of the class, he settled his enormous bulk into a chair, which protested at being required to bear such a heavy burden.

"Good morning, men," he said in a too typically military fashion. "My name is Colonel Frack, U.S. Army, retired."

He spoke as if he was addressing the troops before storming the beach at Normandy.

"I hope you men are finding your way around on your first day here at S.I.L. You look like a fine group of young men, and I look forward to giving you the tools you will need to go out into the world and be good citizens, strong men, and maybe even soldiers. In Military class you will learn such useful skills as first aid, map reading, military bearing, and you'll even learn to shoot a rifle."

What?

"You will also spend two days out of the week learning to march in formation as part of a squad, a company, and a battalion. On the two days of the week when we will be marching, you will be expected to be in uniform."

That's right! We get uniforms!

"Now, if you will all follow me, I will show you the way to the shooting range and then you will be issued your uniforms." With a great deal of difficulty, he hauled his massive frame out of the chair and marched out of the room. We followed him down the hall, where he turned into a door on his right.

We all crammed ourselves into a room that would've made a great bowling alley. It was long and narrow, with cement walls. Only one-fifth of the room was accessible, since the rest of the room was blocked off with sandbags. It was clear that this was the shooting range. It seemed that the shooters would line up next to each other either standing, kneeling, or lying down and shoot at targets that were suspended at the far end of the room.

"This is the shooting range," said Colonel Frack. "Here you will learn to shoot the M-16 rifle. But that won't be for a few weeks yet." The class looked impressed. And I noticed that a couple of the students looked a little too eager. Like maybe they were already making plans to climb the nearest clock tower.

Colonel Frack then led us to the supply room, where Sargent Rodriguez (the supply clerk) issued us everything we needed for that fashionable soldier look—olive-green wool pants, khaki short-sleeve shirts (summer), light green long-sleeve shirts and olive-green wool jackets (winter), black web belts with brass buckles, various patches and brass pins to adorn our shirts, and black, low-quarter leather shoes.

I was a little disappointed about the shoes. I had seen pictures in the school brochure of students in uniform and they were wearing black leather combat boots. I had assumed that we would all get those. Maybe they were for members of the drill teams. For cool factor, the low-quarter shoes were the equivalent of driving a station wagon when all I really wanted was a sports coupe.

STATION WAGON   SPORTS COUPÉ

"Wearing of uniforms will commence next week," said Colonel Frack, "after we have had a chance to instruct you on how to properly wear and maintain them. That's all we have time for today. Good luck, men. And welcome to St. Ignatius Loyola." He dismissed us with a salute.

Biology was taught by Brother Clive, who was British. And I swear as we came into his classroom he stared at every boy's ass as if he wanted to reach out and grab it.

After Bio I had a study period and then lunch. Stuart and I sat at a round table in the corner, comparing classes.

"I can't believe we don't have a thingle clath together," he said. "Although I think you're right. Brother Clive ith a pervert."

Algebra was taught by Brother Eugene, who spoke in one long, continuous sentence without stopping from the beginning of the period until the end.

American History was taught by a lay teacher (meaning he didn't belong to the Jesuits, he was just an ordinary person). His name was Mr. Collier, and I found out later that he also taught Physical Education, coached football, and couldn't spell to save his life.

Religion was taught by Brother Sullivan, who couldn't have been more than twenty-two. He was everything you would expect from a Religion teacher. He was gentle and soft-spoken and he had kind eyes.

All in all it was a pretty run-of-the-mill lot. So far it seemed that Loyola wasn't so different from any other school, although to be fair I don't suppose judging after only one day was giving it a fair and impartial chance. And maybe my fears from my encounter that morning would prove to be unfounded.

Ha.

Once classes were dismissed on that first day I sat on the front steps of the school for over two hours. This is not because I was some great thinker, or because I was pouting or something. It was just because I had to wait until my mom was out of work and she could come pick me up.

As I sat there, I watched the other boys leave. Stuart gave me a friendly wave that somehow didn't seem to match his sour expression. The rest of the boys left and I was there all alone.

I watched the cars go by and I thought about what being at this school was going to mean. I was pretty sure it wasn't going to be any kind of salvation. After all, I was still the same person I was before. I suppose I couldn't expect some magical transformation just because I was in a different place. People were pretty much the same all over the place, weren't they? The boys at Loyola might be a little smarter, but that didn't necessarily make them any nicer. And it certainly didn't guarantee any change in the general opinion toward people who were—different.

The crucial question was this: Was it still going to be a hell on Earth? Or would I at least be allowed to mind my own business, go to class, and get a good education without being tortured on a daily basis? That was the question, wasn't it? How many of the other boys would be like Alejandro Taylor? And here was a new thought: Would there be anyone here like me?

Aha! Maybe that was what was at the root of everything.

In my last school I always saw boys passing notes to girls they liked or girls passing notes to boys they liked. Boys "went" with the girls they liked and vice versa. We even had a couple of school dances. There were match ups and breakups on a weekly, sometimes daily basis. And it made me mad that I couldn't have the same thing, too. The "normal" kids got all the great stuff (and the crappy stuff) that went with romance. And I got none of that. Sitting here in front of the school, I had a lot of time to think. And the more I thought about it, the more I thought that the romance thing was at the root of most of my unhappiness. There was no one I could like who would like me back. And it just wasn't fair.

My mom picked me up at five-twenty. I guess the after-school wait was going to be something to look forward to. I got in the car and strapped myself in.

"So how did it go?" my mother asked.

"Okay."

"Just okay? How are your classes? Did you meet anybody interesting? Details, I want details."

I told her all about my day as we made the twenty-five minute drive home. She asked a couple of questions and then we fell quiet for a few moments as I looked out the window. (This was another great thing about my mom. She didn't feel the need to fill every moment with pointless chatter.)

After a few minutes I turned to face her.

"Mom?"

"Yeah, sweetie?"

"Do you think I'm weird?" She turned to look at me.

"What?"

"Do you think I'm weird?"

"Did somebody tell you that?" she asked, sternly.

"No," I lied. "I'm just curious if you think I'm strange or— you know—a freak."

"Do I think you're weird." She thought for a moment. "Yes. Absolutely. I believe that I can truly say that I have never met anyone like you."

Neither of us spoke for a moment.

"Actually," she said, "it's my favorite thing about you. You are truly one of a kind. And it kind of astounds me that I made a kid like you. I think I can safely say that you are the best thing I have ever done."

We finished the ride in silence.

and then there was
chapter five

Day two at Loyola started in a completely different way. The rest of the students were in the school.

The hallways were crowded with boys in grades nine through twelve, reconnecting, telling stories about what happened over the summer, horsing around, occasionally tussling with one another. It was completely overwhelming to my senses to see so many young men all in one place. It was a little like that dream some kids have of being locked overnight in a candy shop. The upperclassmen were handsome and masculine and well groomed. They had lost that little boy quality to their faces and instead seemed mature and square jawed and confident. The freshmen wandered among them looking small and soft and out of place.

Try as I might, I couldn't help staring at these older boys as they passed me in the halls and on the stairs. It wasn't just that they had handsome faces, but they looked intelligent and grown-up. They smiled and laughed in an easy, self-assured way that made even the homeliest of them intriguing. What was it like? It was like—I don't know. Wait, yes I do. Their presence was intoxicating. I felt a little dizzy and light-headed as I walked up the stairs to my homeroom on the third floor.

Suddenly I saw one boy coming down the stairs towards me. He was tall and broad shouldered, with very blond hair and green eyes. His face was classically handsome with a square jaw and an aristocratic nose. And he wore the full summer JROTC uniform, right down to the black polished combat boots that were worn by the members of the drill team. As I looked up from his boots, I saw his eyes on me, and a sneer of contempt on his face.

"What the hell are you looking at, faggot?" he said, his eyes burning into me. I recoiled as if he had slapped me. He gave a short bark of a laugh and pushed past me, nearly knocking me over.

When I came into homeroom, I saw Brother Marvin off to one side, talking to a group of boys from the class. Stuart was already seated at his desk. Thankfully there was no sign of Alejandro Taylor. I sat down behind Stuart.

"Good morning, Charleth," he said, turning around to look at me. "Ready for your firtht real day?"

"I guess so—" I stopped short as I saw Alejandro come into the room. He stalked down the aisle, pushing past our seats.

"Don't let me interrupt your little tea party," he said nastily.

"What are you talking about?" Stuart asked.

"Ignore him," I said. "He's a jerk."

Alejandro grabbed me by the back of the neck.

"Listen to me, you little pussy. If you know what's good for you, you'll watch that mouth of yours. Unless you want it busted." He shoved me away from him and I nearly fell out of my desk. Brother Marvin looked over.

"*Gentlemen, is there a problem?*"

"No, Brother," I said quickly. "Everything's fine." I straightened myself out and sat back in my desk.

"What'th hith problem?" Stuart whispered to me after Brother Marvin had looked away and Alejandro was talking to the boy behind him.

"Never mind," I said.

Once homeroom was over, I remembered to be excited. Today I would find out what this whole English class thing from yesterday was all about. As the homeroom students filed out, I stayed in my seat, looking to Brother Marvin for some kind of clue. But he actually left the room and stood in the hallway, overseeing the students like a traffic cop as they passed to their next classes.

As the boys began to come into the classroom, I noticed that they all seemed to be older boys. As more and more upperclassmen came in, I began to get more and more nervous that I had made some kind of mistake. Then a couple of girls from St. Cecilia's came in. They wore short plaid pleated skirts and white blouses with short sleeves. Everyone in the class seemed to know one another, and they sat in little groups, talking and laughing. I was clearly in the wrong place.

Brother Marvin came in and stood at his desk, looking over his grade book. I tiptoed up to him, trying to make myself as small as possible.

"Brother Marvin, I think I'm in the wrong place."

"*Nothing to worry about, Charles. You're in the right place. Just have a seat and I'll explain everything as soon as class begins.*" He went back to his grade book.

I went back to my seat and sat squirming, waiting for the bell to ring. This could not be good. The next moment I knew it was going to be terrible.

I saw the boy who had called me a faggot that morning come into the room.

He marched in like he owned the place, saying hi to several people, his back straight and a perpetual smirk on his lips. It was clear he was the head rooster in the barnyard, and this became even clearer when he walked up to the girls from

St. Cecilia's. As he walked up to them, they looked at him like he was some kind of rock star. He stood talking to them, his hands on his hips, which were cocked in a casually cool way. He smiled down at them with a toothy grin and they looked up at him adoringly, like he was the Second Coming. Even though I tried not to, I knew exactly how they felt.

Just as the bell rang, one last girl from St. Cecilia's came into the room. She was very short, her hair long and straight and flaming red. And she had the biggest eyes I had ever seen. There was something startling about the way she looked, but I couldn't put my finger on it. She sat right in the front row.

When she came in, the other students took their seats, and I noticed the blond boy who had called me a faggot just as he noticed me. His winning smile died on his lips and he glared at me as he strolled easily to his seat.

"*Good morning, ladies and gentlemen. Welcome back. I'm very pleased to begin what I know will be another great year in Creative Writing.*" Creative Writing!

"Brother Marvin?" It was the blond boy.

"*Yes, Mr. Schwarz?*" It was clear Brother Marvin was irritated by the interruption.

Blond Schwarz stood up and addressed Brother Marvin and the entire class.

"I'm sorry to interrupt, but I was just wondering what that," he pointed directly at me, "was doing in here with us."

"*I tell you what, Mr. Schwarz. If you will allow me to continue with my introduction, I'm sure all your questions will be answered. Why don't you exhibit a little patience, Dieter, and park your ass in a chair until I'm finished.*"

The other students in the class burst out laughing as Dieter Schwarz turned beet red and then slowly sat down. As he did, he shot me a murderous glance that needed no interpretation.

"Now, if I may continue? I know that most of you know one another, but as Mr. Schwarz pointed out, we have a slightly unexpected member in our class this year. As all of you know, Creative Writing is normally only open to juniors and seniors. Those of you who are seniors this year are returning from Creative Writing class last year, and the juniors all know each other from English II last year. But we do have a member of the class who does not meet this prerequisite."

I felt all the eyes of the students in the class turn to me. At that moment I could have very cheerfully crawled into a hole, if one had opened up in the floor anywhere near me, and pulled the hole in on top of me.

"I would like to introduce you all to Mr. Charles Siskin. He is a newly admitted freshman here at Loyola, and he will be joining the class at my directive. As all the boys at Loyola know, when you take the exam to be admitted to the school, you are required to submit a writing sample. Mr. Siskin submitted a short story that he had written, and it was clear to me that he has the abilities, the creativity, and the talent necessary to excel in this class."

There was a low, slightly hostile murmur that spread across the classroom.

"Well, let's hear it." Dieter said.

"I'm sorry, Mr. Schwarz?"

"If this story is so amazing and incredible, maybe we should all hear it. I, for one, would like to be the judge of whether this so-called masterpiece is really all that fantastic."

"Good god, Dieter. Why don't you put a sock in it?" It was the girl from St. Cecilia's with the red hair.

"Fortunately for us all, Mr. Schwarz, your opinion is not the one that counts under these circumstances. It is my decision to make."

The class "ooohed" as one.

"But, if Mr. Siskin is willing, I would be happy to share it with you."

The entire class turned to me, their eyes boring into my skull.

I opened my mouth, but no sound came out. My lips just gulped like a fish gasping for oxygen.

"Wait!" said Dieter, "I think he's trying to tell us something!"

The tension of the moment broke with the laughter of the class.

"That will be enough. I believe we are focusing too much attention on Mr. Siskin so early in the class. Perhaps once he has gotten to know us a little better, he will feel more comfortable sharing his work with us."

"Tough luck, Sissykins," said Dieter. "We all have to share our writing with the class." Dieter turned his arrogant smirk on me.

"I'm sure no one would deny Mr. Siskin a modicum of latitude in this matter. Let's move on to other things. Mr. Schwarz, you may see me after class. Now, for the first assignment of the year—"

I heaved a sigh of relief as Brother Marvin went on to describe the assignment. The other students turned away from me, and I melted down into my seat, almost crying with relief. After a moment I was able to compose myself and look up from the floor. Dieter Schwarz was piercing me with the slitting eyes of a snake.

When class was over I waited in my desk as long as I could, to avoid running into Dieter. But he was standing right at the front of the room at Brother Marvin's desk. It looked like Brother Marvin was quietly ripping him a new one. Finally Dieter stormed out of the classroom. I waited a moment longer, then headed to the door. As I passed Brother Marvin's desk, he put a hand on my shoulder.

"I'm sorry, Charles. I hope I didn't embarrass you too much. I just wanted you and the rest of the class to know that I think you have exceptional talent. And Mr. Schwarz aside, I'm sure you will fit in quite nicely here. I'm very glad to have you in my class, and I look forward to reading more of your work." He smiled warmly at me as I blushed and backed toward the door.

"Thank you, Brother Marvin," I managed to mumble as I left the classroom.

My warm feelings were short-lived. As I left the classroom, Dieter and some other students were still standing around in the hall.

"Hey, Sissykins," Dieter growled at me. "If you're really as brilliant as Brother says, you'll have the sense to stay out of my way." He marched past me, shoving me with his shoulder into a row of lockers.

"Are you okay?" It was the girl from St. Cecilia's with the red hair.

"I'm fine," I said, straightening my shirt and picking up my satchel.

"Don't pay any attention to Herr Schwarz," she said, smiling. "I'm not sure, but I think his parents were in the SS." She turned smartly on her heel, tossing her hair. Her plaid skirt swirled prettily as she walked away.

the story

The Scratching in the Walls

He had emerged without so much as a bruise from the accident that had killed his wife and his four-year-old son. The accident that had taken his family away from him had left him completely unharmed, physically. What it had done to his heart and to his soul was another matter entirely.

Unable to face the idea of waking up in the same house that had held the three of them, of walking on the floors that had been polished by their six stockinged feet, of eating breakfast at their table, of sleeping under the roof that had protected them from the rain, he sold the house and moved several hundred miles away.

The real estate agent had tried to discourage him from looking at this new house. He had seen the listing almost by accident as he stood in her office, staring at her bulletin board. Buried under the listings for new condominiums with amenities and townhouses with garden yards was the forgotten, neglected listing for this house. The paper of the listing was curled at the edges and yellow with age and dust. "Stunning Victorian, three bedroom, two bath, living room, parlor, large kitchen, formal dining room, attic space and basement suitable for finishing: $100,000." The listing was dated seven years previous.

"It's totally unsuitable for your needs," the agent had said. "I mean, what on earth are you going to do with so much room? And it's been on the market forever. I haven't even shown the place in at least five years. It's probably falling apart."

But he insisted and she reluctantly agreed to show it to him.

When he saw the house, he fell immediately in love. True, it needed a few repairs, but nothing so major that they could not be dealt with. But even as he walked through the house, the agent did her best to discourage him.

"A house this big will be tough to keep up," she said. "The kitchen will need new appliances. And the whole house needs to be painted, inside and out. These floors could stand to be refinished."

"Well, with a pitch like that," he replied, "it is a wonder it hasn't sold before now." She had the decency to look a bit embarrassed. "Now tell me, honestly," he continued, "what have you got against this house?"

She bit her lip. "Nothing. Nothing, really," she insisted. "I mean every old house has a past, hasn't it?" She walked through the kitchen and opened the door to the back yard. "The yard will need to be redone," she said, trying to change the subject.

"Alright," he said firmly, walking up to her and shutting the door to the back yard. "Out with it."

The agent sighed and then spoke very quickly. "The previous owners were a husband and wife with a young daughter. Five or six, I think she was. They sold the house and moved away right after the child died."

"Died of what?" he asked.

"Bacterial meningitis. Took her so fast they didn't even have time to get her to the hospital. She died right in the house."

He moved in two months later.

The inside and the outside had been painted, the floors sanded and polished, new appliances installed in the kitchen and the front and back yards completely landscaped. When everything was finished, it was the most beautiful house he had ever seen. On the evening of the day he moved in, he sat at the dining room table eating his meal for one and he toasted the beginning of what he hoped would be a new and happier life.

He heard the scratching in the walls on the first night.

He lay in bed, in the dark, unable to sleep, when he heard the faintest of scratching sounds coming from the front of the house. His bedroom was at the back of the house and the other two bedrooms were at the front. The bedroom to the right of the hall was a typical, rectangular room. The room to the left was in the turret of the house and was completely round. As of yet, there was no furniture in the room. The scratching seemed to be coming from this room.

He walked barefoot down the hall but before he could get to the door of the room, the scratching stopped. He continued to the room, opened the door and stepped inside. It was quiet and even his bare footfalls echoed with the emptiness of the room. There were no coverings on the windows, and the light from the streetlamp came streaming in, bathing the room in a cold, bluish light. It was completely silent.

Great, he thought to himself. There must be rats living in the walls.

"I'll get some traps tomorrow," he said out loud. The sound of his voice was unnerving in the empty room, and he quickly left the room and went back to bed.

The next day he got some traps and placed them around the house, including in the closet of the turret room. But despite this, the traps yielded nothing and the scratching sound continued every night, quiet and gentle and stopping whenever he came near.

As the days went past he decided that if the rats weren't going to bother him, he wouldn't bother them. He set the other bedroom up as a guest room, and the turret room he furnished as his office, with desk, chairs, an old wood filing cabinet and a small love seat. He found the room oddly comforting, and spent a great deal of time in there, even though he really only needed the room for paying bills or writing letters. There seemed to be a perpetual comforting scent in the room of talcum powder and wild flowers.

It was in the second week that he began to hear the footsteps.

Often, when he was on the first floor, he would hear the sound of footsteps causing the floorboards to creak slightly. He would hear this sound, as if someone was walking around in the turret room above his head, and then the footsteps would stop when he got to the bottom of the stairs.

At the end of the second week, he was coming in from the grocery store when he heard the faint sound of a child's laughter coming from the upstairs hall. He froze in the kitchen, standing perfectly still and clutching a paper bag of groceries to his chest. He heard more footsteps from above and then fainter laughter from the turret room. He dropped the bag of groceries when he heard the door to the turret room slam shut.

The following Monday he went to the real estate office to see the agent who had sold him the house. He sat in her office, sipping coffee as she sat across her desk from him, moving papers around on the desk in a pointless and nervous manner.

"So!" she said, with a bit too much false cheer in her voice, "How are things going at the house?" He noticed that she never looked directly at him.

"Well, the house is beautiful. Everything turned out exactly as I wanted."

"Wonderful," she said. A heavy moment of silence sat between them. "Is there something I can do for you? Is something wrong?" she said after a long moment.

"Well, I know that the house stood empty for quite a while. And you had said that you hadn't even shown it for at least five years." He shifted in his seat.

"That's right."

"Is there anything else you haven't told me?"

"Anything else? Anything like what?"

"Well there must be some reason you stopped showing the house. After all, it's not like the place was a total wreck. It's in a good neighborhood and was listed at a great price. Just because a child died in the house is no reason for it to have sat empty for so long." He looked intently at her, waiting for a response.

Finally she said, "Well, I did actually rent the property out once before, several years ago. But the occupants didn't stay for very long. They complained that they heard noises in the house, scratching in the walls and such. They moved out after only a week. At the time I thought it was pretty silly, but after that no one seemed to show any interest in the place. Several people commented that the house gave them the chills. And I do confess that I never felt very comfortable when I was alone in the house. But these kinds of thoughts are ridiculous, aren't they? After a while I just stopped showing the place and there it sat." She looked at him directly for the first time. "Is there some kind of problem with the house?"

He looked directly back at her for a long moment, and then abruptly stood up to leave.

"No," he said, "Nothing at all."

Several weeks went by and he seemed to grow accustomed to the sounds he heard. It was almost like having a roommate that he never saw. He spoke to no one about the noises, and deep down in his heart he began to feel some sort of affection for the presence that shared his house.

One night he sat at his desk in the turret room, some classical music playing softly on the stereo. After a time he went over to the closet and brought down a box that he had placed up on the shelf of the closet when he first moved in. He took the box to the desk and opened it, taking out several framed photographs and two photo albums. He set the photos up on the desk and then sat down at the desk with the albums in front of him.

He sat there for a very long time, looking at the framed pictures on the desk and then at the cover of the photo albums. After a long moment he opened the first album. A photo of an infant was on the first page.

He looked at the photo for a long time, and then he spoke quietly: "This is my son, Alex," he said. "We took this picture on the day we brought him home from the hospital."

He turned the page. "This is my wife, Virginia. She was the most beautiful woman I have ever known." He turned page after page, explaining each photo aloud to the empty room.

After several pages of photos, tears began to stream down his face and his voice grew husky with emotion as he spoke aloud. When he came to the end of the album, he shut it and sat back at his desk.

As he sat, the scent of talcum powder and wild flowers grew stronger, and he felt from behind him two small arms twine around his shoulders.

It had been months since the real estate agent had heard anything from him, and on a whim she stopped by the house one afternoon when she was in the neighborhood. She knocked at the front door and stood waiting, looking at the manicured front lawn and the well washed windows.

After a moment he opened the door. He looked much the same, except that she noticed a streak of grey in his hair that hadn't been there before, and his eyes seemed very black and deep and distracted.

"Oh, hello," he said. She noticed a slight twitching below his left eye. "I didn't expect any company today."

"Well I would have called," she said, "but it was sort of a spur of the moment thing. I hope I'm not intruding dropping by like this, but I realized that I hadn't heard from you and I was curious to see how you were getting along and what you had done to the place."

"No. No. Not intruding at all. Please come in." His voice was flat and colorless. He showed her around the ground floor and seemed to be ready to guide her back to the front door, when she turned and climbed the stairs.

"It's simply lovely," she said as she reached the top of the stairs. "I'm anxious to see how the room in the turret turned out. Didn't you tell me that you planned on using it as an office?" She headed toward the turret room. He pushed past her quickly as she walked down the hall and shut the door to the turret room before she could reach it.

"Oh, the office turned out fine," he said. "It's just such an ungodly mess in there." He laughed nervously and steered her away from the door.

"Well, I'm so glad everything turned out so well for you here," she said as she stood on the porch about to leave.

"Yes. Everything turned out just fine. Thank you so much for everything." He said, mechanically. He closed the door, leaving her standing on the porch. As she walked to her car, she wiped her brow.

He had shut the door to the office before she could go in, but not before she had seen that the room was not furnished like an office at all.

The room had been painted a pale pink and furnished with a small girl's bed, a white wood dresser and a toy box.

chapter six,
pick up sticks

"Wow, that was really creepy," said Joe Ramirez, a junior in the class.

It was my third week at Loyola and I had finally gotten up the nerve to share with the rest of the class the story that I had submitted as a writing sample.

"I thought it was an interesting choice not to name the main character," said the girl with red hair from St. Cecilia's. Her name was, believe it or not, Phaedre. "I also liked that it didn't go where I thought it was going to go. I thought it was going to be like a haunted house--type story, but it's really a story about loss and about the lengths a person will go to when they have experienced such a tragic event. It makes me wonder how someone so young came up with such a heart wrenching story." She turned around in her desk and smiled at me, then turned around again.

"I thought it was stupid," said Dieter.

"Mr. Schwarz, keep your comments constructive. I don't want to have to warn you again."

"I just don't see what all the fuss is about," he said with an arrogant sneer. "I mean he didn't even finish the story."

"I liked that it had a kind of unfinished quality," said Duane Stemple, a thick-necked sort of hick who was a senior. "I mean I appreciated that he left so much to the reader's imagination. There was a lean, spare sort of feel to his style of writing that reminded me a little of Hemingway."

Dieter snorted in reply, but kept his mouth shut under Brother Marvin's stern glance.

"I think a lot of writers in this class could learn a thing or two about simplifying their writing," said Stacy Ingalls, a junior from St. Cecilia's.

"If you have other comments for Charles, I would encourage you to use the feedback slips. And thank you, Charles, for sharing your work with us. As we continue on in the year, you will see that we use this workshop format regularly, and I encourage you all to offer one another plenty of positive feedback and constructive suggestions so that you can improve on the work that you are doing."

As class was ending a couple of people stopped by my desk and left me feedback notes. As I was gathering my books, Dieter walked up to my desk and stood in front of me, his weight slung over on one leg and one hand on his hip.

"Here, Sissykins," he said, thrusting a feedback sheet at me. "Loved the story. It would make a great comic book." He turned on his heel and sauntered off.

Phaedre came up to me as I was slinging my satchel across my shoulder.

"Is he still bothering you?" she said.

"No," I lied. "He just wanted to give me a feedback slip."

"Well, let me know if he gives you any trouble and I'll kick him in the marbles. Great story, by the way." She slapped a feedback slip on my desk and turned and bounced out of the room.

I sat in the back row of the study hall and laid all four of the feedback slips I had gotten on the desk in front of me.

STORY: The Scratching in the Walls

AUTHOR: Charles Siskin

FEEDBACK: Great story! Nice to have you with us, kid. The ending really surprised me.

BY: Howard Ionazzi

STORY: The Scratching in the Walls

AUTHOR: Charles

FEEDBACK: Very cool stuff. Think about adding more detail, especially a description of what the house looks like.

BY: Amanda

STORY: _The Scratching in the Walls_

AUTHOR: _Charles Sissykins_

FEEDBACK: You're writing sucks my ass and you walk like a girl. When your finished with this feedback maybe you can roll it up and use it as a tampon.

BY: _A Friend_

STORY: _The Scratching in the Walls_

AUTHOR: _Charles Siskin_

FEEDBACK: I think your writing is fantastic! It's amazing to me that someone so young would have so much insight into the human heart. I can't wait to read more.

BY: _Phaedre Brodowski_

At lunch that day I sat with what had become my regular crowd. Stuart, of course, and a couple of other freshmen who had formed a little group of misfits. We sat at the table in the far corner, farthest from the entrance to the cafeteria. This was either because we liked our privacy or because it was a strategic place to keep an eye on the rest of the room and it was almost impossible to sneak up on us there.

The five of us were about as unlikely a group of boys as you could possibly imagine. There was Chris Fleming, who we all called Fritz, because on the day Stuart met him, Stuart had misheard him when he said his name. He had said "Chris" and Stuart had heard "Fritz," and when he introduced him to the group we had a good laugh and of course the name stuck.

There was Jacob Hung, and I'm sure you can guess we all got a big kick out of that name, and Nels Tanner, who wore glasses so thick that he was legally blind without them.

The five of us made a pitiful but loyal little group, bound together by the sheer fact that we were all so odd. We met every morning in the cafeteria before school started and played Spades or sometimes wrote Mad Libs. All of us had a really firm grasp of the ridiculous, and it was clear that no one else wanted to have anything to do with us. So here we sat, linked together by our status as outsiders, assembled on our life raft of a table in the corner of the cafeteria.

"So, guess what I discovered today," said Fritz.

"What?" said Nels, staring at him through his magnifying-lens glasses, which were also smeared with fingerprints.

"Apparently Brother Clive will give you the answers to any question on his quizzes if you let him put his hand on your leg."

"Are you kidding?" said Nels, stuffing French fries in his mouth.

"Yeah. I was taking that quiz on genetics today and I had a problem with one of the questions. So I raised my hand and he came over and kneeled down next to me. I asked him my question, and he put his hand on my thigh. At first I was going to pull away, but then he pointed at the right answer, gave my leg a squeeze and went back to his desk. I tried it again with another question, and he did the same thing."

"Jethuth, what a perv," said Stuart.

"He let me turn in late homework when I let him put his arm around me," said Jacob calmly.

Nels took out his homework notebook and made a quick note in it. "Good to know," he said, and stuffed the notebook back in his bag.

"Yesterday," said Jacob, "I found out that all the upperclassmen call Brother Baker 'Brubaker.' You know, like that warden in that prison movie. To his face! I'm pretty sure Brother Baker doesn't have a clue why they're doing it. I heard a senior say that Brother Baker thought it was some kind of a cool nickname. They call him 'Brubaker' and he blushes, like it was some kind of tribute."

We all laughed.

"Something funny, faggot?" said a junior kid passing by whose name I didn't know. He lobbed his carton of milk at me, hitting me on the shoulder, then kept walking. Everyone just kept eating. It wasn't the first time one of us had been hit by a carton of milk or a donut or even a slice of pizza. And we were all pretty sure it wouldn't be the last.

$^2/_5$ $^3/_5$ $^4/_5$

HARM INFLICTION RATING

"Hey, Charles!" said Nels, suddenly excited. "Listen to this Mad Lib from yesterday":

Letter from Camp

Dear _Aunt Mary Beth_,
(name)

I am having an _ugly_
(adjective)
time at camp. The counselor is fantastic
and the food is_bloated_. I
(adjective)
met _Jacob_ and we became
(name)
tall friends. Unfortunately,
(adjective)
Jacob is _creamy_ and
(name)   (adjective)
I _sucked_ my _butt_
(verb, past tense)   (noun)
so we couldn't go _eating_ like
(verb)
everybody else. I need more _eggs_
(noun, plural)
and a _metaphor_ sharpener, so please
(noun)
quickly _drive_ more when
(adverb)   (verb)
you _crunch_ back.
(verb)

Your _Cousin_,
(relative title)
Stuart
(name)

Sadly, we all burst out laughing and laughed uncontrollably for about five minutes. Pudding came out of Stuart's nose, which made us laugh more. I know, it's stupid. But for me it was priceless. I hadn't had any friends in years, and I couldn't believe how good it felt just to be around people. And to laugh. True, we were a pretty dorky group, but that was kind of the best part. I had my own little clique of outcasts. And we were happy.

At the end of the day I sat in my usual place on the front steps, waiting for my mom to pick me up. Most of the students had left, and I was three chapters into Steinbeck's *East of Eden* when a finger tapped me on the shoulder.

"Howdy, sailor." It was Phaedre.

"Hi."

"Whatcha readin'?"

"*East of Eden.*" I showed her the book cover.

"Lofty. I notice you sit out here a lot. What gives?"

"Oh. I have to wait for my mom to get off work so she can come and pick me up."

"Can't you take the bus home?"

"I don't know. I guess so. I never really thought about it. It would probably worry my mom too much anyway. I live pretty far away."

"Try it sometime," she said, sitting next to me on the steps. "It's got to be better than sitting out here all afternoon."

"Yeah, maybe I will."

We sat a moment in silence.

"Listen," I said, "I want to thank you for what you wrote about my story. It really means a lot to me. Especially coming from you. I mean you really seem to know what you're talking about in class when it comes to writing."

"You're right about that," she said matter-of-factly. The way she said it, it didn't sound conceited at all, just simple and straightforward. "I spend most of my time writing and reading. And I want to study writing in two years when I go to college. Even though my parents keep hounding me to go pre-law."

"Dieter said my writing sucked."

"That douchebag wouldn't know good writing if it bit him on his ass. You may have noticed he hasn't shared anything with the class yet this year. And the stuff he wrote last year was ridiculous. A bunch of sci-fi and fantasy crap about women with three breasts and muscly guys with swords rescuing helpless maidens. Totally *jejune*[9]."

"Jejune?" I said.

"It means dull, juvenile, childish. If you get nothing else out of Brother Marvin's class, you'll come out with a great vocabulary. He may sound like Kermit the Frog, but the man knows more words than Webster."

"Oh my god, he does sound like Kermit the Frog, doesn't he?"

"Completely! The entire first week I had him for class I had to bite my lip to keep from laughing out loud. But he's a fantastic teacher and a total sweetheart. And it's obvious he loves your writing. As far as I know there's never been a freshman admitted to that class. And clearly that's what's got Dieter's panties in a twist. He's completely out of his depth, and he knows it. It's just jealousy, plain and simple. Oh, shit! Here comes my bus." She stood up and brushed off her skirt.

---

[9]**je•june** [*ji-***joon**] *adj.* 1. devoid of significance or interest; dull 2. immature or juvenile, as in behavior 3. uninformed or falling short in knowledge 4. without nutritive worth, as in diet

For a practically grown man, Dieter Schwarz was pitifully jejune.

"Hey, listen Phaedre. Thanks for everything. You made my day."

"Any time, sweet pants!" she yelled over her shoulder as she ran for the bus. I watched her get on and take a seat, then she waved to me from the window as the bus pulled away.

That weekend I went out with Sammy. She had called me up and said she was taking me out to lunch.

Sammy was a lawyer and she had loads of money. So of course she chose a pretty swanky place to eat. I had to get kind of dressed up and we had lunch at a place called the Parkend Grille, which was located, oddly enough, at the end of a park. We sat across the linen covered table from one another, her with a paté in front of her, me with a lobster bisque.

"So, Egghead. How goes the new school?" She signaled the waiter for another glass of wine.

"It's not bad," I said, blowing on my soup.

"Not bad? Is that all? I was expecting to hear rave reviews." She spread some paté on a toast point and jammed it in her mouth.

"No, it's great. Really. I got placed in a creative writing class that's usually only meant for juniors and seniors."

"What?! That's fantastic! That deserves a toast." She snatched the new glass of wine out of the waiter's hand before he could put it on the table. She raised her glass up and I did the same with my iced tea. "To my favorite egghead. I always knew you were destined for greatness."

We clinked glasses and she smiled broadly at me and winked.

After lunch she decided we needed to have dessert at some favorite place of hers she called a "patisserie."

"A special treat for a special day," she said as we walked across the parking lot toward her Mercedes.

"Sammy?" I said, as we strolled along. "Do you think I walk like a girl?"

She looked over at me, lowering her Jackie O sunglasses.

"I don't know, Egghead. I never really thought about it. Do you think you walk like a girl?'

"Well, I'm definitely not the most manly guy in the world." I said.

She snorted a short laugh.

"Well, if you want to walk more like a man walk like me. My mother always said I had a mannish walk."

"How's a man supposed to walk?" I asked.

She thought for a moment. "I don't know. Open your legs more," she finally said. "Walk like your balls are too big for you." She opened her legs and adopted an old western kind of stance. We walked across the parking lot like two gunslingers ready for a shoot-out.

ground control
to chapter seven

As the days and weeks slipped past, I developed a real love--hate relationship with St. Ignatius Loyola High School. It seemed like every time something great happened, something shitty would happen to balance things out. If everything had been great I could have gone on from now until forever. If everything had been shitty I might've gone to my parents, admitted I had made a mistake and asked to transfer to James Madison (or run off and joined the circus).

But it seemed like being at Loyola was an endless roller coaster of highs and lows.

High: I had made some friends who I could hang out with on a daily basis. Stuart, Jacob, Fritz, Nels, and I spent all of our downtime together. In the morning we all usually got to the school at least a half hour early and spent that time playing Uno or Spades in the cafeteria (or sometimes writing MadLibs). We ate lunch together every day. Even though we all lived in separate parts of the city, we had managed to get together a couple of times for a movie or to hang out at a mall like normal kids. I even spent the night at Stuart's house once. We watched *The Omen* on TV and scared the shit out of each other after it was over, and stayed up late drawing caricatures of our least favorite boys and teachers at the school. We started out with drawings, then made collage figures using pictures we had cut out of a stack of his mother's magazines. Of course there came a time during the course of the evening when we dragged out the school directory and made prank calls to several of the worst jackweeds that St. Ignatius Loyola had to offer (May I speak to Jean Yussiss? I'm sorry, there's no Jean Yussiss here. Oh, only idiots like you?). At one point we were laughing so hard Stuart actually peed his pj's a little and had to change into another pair. Oh! And also, I turned fourteen! I had a birthday in November and I got together with my little group of misfits for a birthday celebration at an ice cream parlor called "Klondike's." We stuffed ourselves with banana splits and hot fudge sundaes and spent three bucks playing ridiculous songs on their fantastically out of date juke box. Stuart played this truly horrible song called "Tiny Bubbles" by some guy named Don Ho at least three times.

Low: Some unnamed vandal poured superglue into the lock on my locker and wrote "queer" on the front with indelible marker. I found it after Military class one day when I came up to my locker to get my book for Religion. There was a crowd of boys standing around my locker when I got there, laughing, and when they saw me they parted like the Red Sea. When I saw that word written in bold black letters on the locker door, I scanned the crowd to see if I could tell if any of the boys there had done it, but I couldn't. The custodian had to paint over it, but it stayed up there for two days.

High: Brother Marvin had taken me under his wing and my writing and vocabulary were improving with great *alacrity*[10] (see?). I presented another story to the class and it was really well received, and I got a ton of positive feedback about it. I didn't even get a hate note from Dieter the Wonder-Nazi.

Low: J.J. Barker, a school bully with a promising career as a petty thug and potential convict punched me in the stomach at a school dance. I had never even spoken to the guy (a sophomore) before. As near as I can figure, he was pissed off because I was dancing with a group of girls from St. Cecilia's. Stuart said "He'th probably jutht jealouth becauthe you were danthing with all thothe girlth and no girl in her right mind would ever danthe with him becauthe he lookth like he hath an exthra chromothome."

High: Phaedre and I had become really good friends, and through her I got to know a lot of really cool girls at St. Cecilia's. None of these girls seemed to care what my voice sounded like or how I walked, and they appreciated my fashion sense. And Phaedre and I talked together a lot, about writing and life and important things, unlike most of my peers, who seemed to be obsessed with trivial things like how many chicks they had banged or getting wasted at some stereotypical party (which I never got invited to anyway). We confided in one another. One day I worked up my courage and told her that I liked boys, and without missing a beat she said, "Really? Give me a list of your top five favorite sexy boys at Loyola."

---

[10]**a•lac•ri•ty** [*uh*-**lak**-ri-tee] *n.* 1. promptness in response 2. cheerful liveliness or readiness

I used this word with Coach Collier once and he looked at me like I had sprouted a second head.

Low: I pretty much got called gay or fag or queer or homo or pansy or butt pirate or some other slur on a daily basis. And the thing that really got me about that was that I technically wasn't really gay. I mean I hadn't really done anything with another guy. Although to be totally fair, I guess I was bringing it on myself. I knew that I sounded like a queer. My voice was soft and high and womanly. And I videotaped myself walking and it was true. I walked like a girl. Sammy's walking lesson had helped a little, but I was effeminate. There was no getting around it.

To add to that I seemed to insist on staring at cute boys. I just couldn't help myself. My hormones seemed to be in total control of my body, and when a handsome boy walked by me, I slurped him up with my eyes. I couldn't stop myself from visually worshipping a handsome face or a great pair of eyes or tasty looking lips or tight-muscled bodies. And with hot guys running around in military uniforms all over the place, can you really blame me? And if you think that high school-age boys at an all-boys military Catholic high school don't know when someone is staring at them; you'd be sadly mistaken. They caught me every time. And about 70% of the time that was where the getting called gay, fag, queer, etc. usually followed.

I couldn't even stop myself from giving Dieter Schwarz, the bane of my existence, the once over when I knew he wasn't looking. True, he was an asshole. But in some sick kind of a way, that was part of what made him so attractive. Plus he had a great ass.

So, in any event, time marched on. And every time I thought I wouldn't be able to take the torment another day, something great would come along and make it all bearable. All of this leads me to the two major events that I wanted to

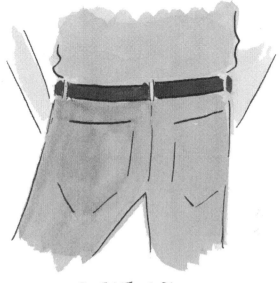

GREAT ASS

make sure I included in this epic tale. The first was only semi-major and had to do with a bar.

Around the middle of the school year my mom had to go out of town for some training seminar for her job. She and my dad were trying to figure out the best way to get me to and from school.

"It's just so damned inconvenient," my dad said. "I mean I work five minutes from home, which means I'll have to drive all the way downtown to drop you off or pick you up and then drive home again. Not to mention that it's going to add almost an hour to your usual wait time after school."

"Well it's only for a week," my mom said, "and I don't see any other way around it."

"Why don't I just take the bus?" I said.

"I don't know about that," my mom replied, her brow furrowed with concern. "It's such a long way, and I'd be worried sick about you the whole time."

"Practically every other kid takes the bus," I said. "I'm pretty much the only person in the whole school who waits to be picked up. And it would only be for a week. And I could call Dad as soon as I got home."

"Do you even know which bus to take?" my father asked.

I had already been doing my research on this very topic.

"Dad can drop me off in the morning at Woodcreek Mall. I catch the 648 into downtown and then transfer to the 62, which stops right in front of the school. After school it's just the reverse and then a ten minute walk home."

"Apparently you've done your homework," my mother said, suspiciously.

"Come on, Mom. I'm fourteen years old and I'm totally capable of taking a bus home."

My parents looked at each other for a long minute.

"We could have him do a dry run this Friday and see if everything works out okay," said my dad. Yea, Dad!

"Well, I guess if it's only for a week it will be alright," my mom grudgingly replied. "But only for that week and only if the dry run goes smoothly."

The dry run went off without a hitch, and finally my first day of pseudo-adulthood arrived. My mom had left town the night before, kissing me several times and giving me a verbal list of warnings about keeping my eyes open and not talking to strangers and keeping my wallet in my front pocket and sticking by other students from the school as much as possible and coming right home and calling my dad as soon as I got home and on and on and on.

So I took the bus to school the next day and arrived with more than twenty minutes to spare. When school ended that Monday, I got on one of the buses that stopped in front of the school with the rest of the boys from Loyola and the girls from St. Cecilia's. These buses were public buses, but at this time of day they were completely filled with students from the two schools. I had seen them when I sat on the front steps waiting for my mom to come pick me up, and I knew that they were crowded, but seeing them from the front steps of the school was nothing like actually riding on one.

The bus was so packed with students it was like half-price day in the New Delhi open market. And there was so much noise I thought my brain was going to come leaking out of my ears. And because it was all students, it was kind of like they had imported one of the hallways between classes from inside the building onto a moving vehicle. Since I had been so anxious and excited about riding the bus, I had run out of the building and managed to get a seat for Phaedre and me near the back.

The bus pulled away from the curb and began the trip into the downtown area. As Phaedre and I sat trying to hear each other over the din, I noticed that Alejandro Taylor was sitting a few rows ahead of us. He's the boy who sat behind me in homeroom and called me a pansy on the first day of school. Since that first day he had ignored me most of the time, although every once in a while he was pleasant enough to greet me in the morning with "good morning pansy," or occasionally on a Monday he might ask me if me and my girlfriend (he meant Stuart) had gone out on a date on Saturday.

The trip into the downtown area was actually pretty short, maybe about fifteen minutes. We were one stop away from where I had to get off and transfer to the bus that would take me out to the mall. The majority of the students had already gotten off the bus one stop before, so the noise had subsided to a dull roar.

"Hey, pansy!" yelled Alejandro Taylor back to me. "Shouldn't you get off here? You can stop in for a drink and a quickie in the bathroom before you go home." He and his friends erupted into loud, obnoxious laughter. I was so used to being taunted like this that I didn't even get mad.

"Do you know what he's talking about?" I asked Phaedre.

"Oh, he's probably talking about that bar there." She pointed out the window to a low building made of pink brick.

An unlit neon sign outside said "Auntie Dick's." Aside from this, the building was extremely nondescript and the door was a discreet, unmarked black.

"It's a gay bar. He's just being an asshole." Phaedre said. "Hey, shit for brains!" she yelled up to him. "Did your mother have any children that lived?" His friends erupted in even

louder laughter, and a couple of them threw some paper at his head. His face got bright red and he turned back around to face the front of the bus, trying to pretend that nothing had happened.

As the bus continued on its way, I snuck a last look out the window at Auntie Dick's.

By Tuesday I had convinced myself that I needed to go inside that bar. It was like there was something drawing me there. I needed to see what it was like inside. Maybe it was kind of like the creation story that we had studied in Brother Sullivan's Religion class. In the middle of the Garden of Eden stood the Tree of the Knowledge of Good and Evil. And in spite of God's warning not to eat of the fruit, Eve was drawn to it and unable to resist the temptation when the serpent coaxed her to eat of the fruit of the tree. And even though I knew that it turned out pretty badly for Adam and Eve, I couldn't pry my mind away from it.

On Wednesday and Thursday I thought I had worked up my nerve, but I chickened out at the very last second. When Friday came, I knew it would probably be my last chance to see the inside of this place for a while. I got off the bus at my regular downtown stop, said good-bye to Phaedre and pretended to go into a corner grocery for some gum. After walking around in there for ten minutes, I slipped out of the store like a foreign spy, looking up and down the street for any signs of Loyola boys or St. Cecilia girls. Then I walked quickly with my head down the two bus stops back to Auntie Dick's.

I was sure that the place would be closed, but when I tried the door it was open. With my heart hammering a mile a minute, I slipped inside.

It took me several minutes for my eyes to adjust to the dim interior.

I'm not sure what I expected to find there. I think I had convinced myself that it would be a little like Dante's Inferno, with half-naked bodies of muscled men writhing around to a heavy disco beat. I would worm my way through their twisting bodies and belly up to the bar and order a Harvey Wallbanger. I would lean against the bar coolly sipping my drink and surveying the patrons of the bar with a detached and smooth air. After a moment, a shirtless, muscled, oily man with a shaved head and a tattoo of an anchor on his chest would come up to me and fix me with a steely gaze. Then he'd grab the back of my head and roughly kiss me on the mouth. We would dance for an hour before he'd give me a ride home on the back of his Harley Davidson motorcycle. Then I would spend the whole weekend in my room playing our time together over and over again while I did my Biology homework.

I don't think you'll be surprised to hear that it was nothing like that.

The whole space was one small room, with a jukebox in one corner, a bar to the right and a pool table at the back. The bar was paneled in cheap, dark imitation wood paneling and there were maybe four or five tables scattered around the place. The tables had those candles in red glass jars with netting around them.

The bar was completely empty except for four people: the bartender, two guys sitting at the bar, and me. The bartender was probably forty or so, portly in build and sporting a crew cut. He looked like he ran a green grocery. The two patrons were both at least sixty years old and sat hunched over their drinks, each smoking a cigarette. Not one of them looked over at me when I came into the bar.

Once my eyes had adjusted to the gloom, I walked into the center of the room. I stood there for what seemed like an hour, just looking around at this disappointing excuse for a pit of sin. After what was probably actually less than two minutes, I heard a voice from my left.

"Are you lost, kid?" It was the bartender. He was leaning forward on the bar and the two retirees had spun around on their barstools and were looking at me.

I stood there staring at them with my mouth open.

"Did you hear me, kid? Do you need something?" the bartender said, speaking more loudly.

I adopted a quick air of nonchalance and moseyed over to the bar like I was John Wayne in an old western.

"Sure," I said casually. "Lemme have a beer." I had never had a beer in my entire life.

The retirees looked over at the bartender and he gave them a quick glance, barely able to suppress a smile.

"Right," he said. "A beer. What kind?" He looked straight at me, his brows raised in mock expectation.

"What kind? Ummm . . . how about a Bud?" It was the first commercial that popped into my head.

"One Bud, coming right up." He grinned at the two retirees and grabbed a glass from the shelf behind him. He walked over to the tap and held the glass under the spout, then stopped suddenly. "Say," he said, "I don't suppose you have any I.D. on you? Normally I wouldn't ask, but you do look kind of young." The two retirees choked back a laugh and stared down onto their drinks.

"I.D.?" I sputtered. "Ummmm . . . I think I must've left it at home. I'm not really used to getting carded."

"How old are you anyway, kid?" The bartender asked.

"How old am I? Twenty-two. And a half." Clearly

the addition of "a half" would make my ridiculous lie absolutely believable.

"Is that so?" He looked over at the retirees, who were barely able to hold back their laughter. "You don't look a day over twenty." The three of them burst out laughing.

"Seriously, kid," the bartender said after all three had had a really good chuckle. "You couldn't be more than, what? Fifteen, tops?"

I looked down at the worn maroon carpet, blushing, then turned slowly and headed toward the door.

"Hey, kid!" The bartender called out to me, but his tone had softened and he smiled warmly at me when I turned. "What are you doing in here, anyway?"

I had to fight hard to keep my voice from quaking. For some reason I was very close to crying.

"I . . . I just wanted to see . . . I just wanted to see what it was like inside. I'm sorry. I didn't mean to cause any trouble."

"Aw, c'mon, Chet." It was one of the retirees. "Let the kid look around."

"Shut your trap, Bob. I'm sorry, kid. But I could lose my liquor license."

"Like there's any chance of anyone besides us coming in here at this time of day," said Bob.

"Have a heart, Chet," said the other retiree. "The kid just wants to look around. Right, kid?"

"No, he's right. I shouldn't have come in here in the first place. It was stupid." I turned again to go.

"Alright, alright," said Chet. "I can handle anything but a scene from Lassie Come Home. Here, kid." He filled the beer glass with ice and Coca-Cola from the gun by his hand. "One Coke, a quick look around and then beat it. And if you come back before you're nineteen I'll report you to the truant officer." He handed me my Coke. I put my hand in my pocket for some cash.

"How much do I owe you?" I said.

"This one's on me," Chet replied.

"Thanks, Chet." I said. The two old geezers at the bar looked at each other and cackled.

I turned away from the bar and took in the empty room. Now what? I thought. The place was completely deserted and I had already seen the whole place. I walked with my Coke over to the jukebox and leaned against it. Chet, Bob, and the other guy were talking quietly among themselves.

I stood there for about ten minutes, sipping my drink. Absolutely nothing happened. Chet, Bob, and the other guy talked. I leaned against the jukebox. Not a soul came in the bar. After a few more minutes, I walked cautiously back to the bar, placing my empty glass down.

"Say, Chet," I said. All three men looked down the bar at me. "Does anyone else ever come in here?" The two retirees burst out laughing.

"That's great, kid," said Chet. "Your first time in a gay bar and you're already busting my balls."

"No, I'm sorry. I don't mean to. I was just wondering where . . . if you get any . . . I mean, there's no one here!" Bob and the other retiree burst out laughing again, louder this time. Bob fell off his barstool. I looked at the three of them, my eyes wide and my mouth open.

"Jesus, kid. It's four o'clock in the afternoon. This place doesn't get going 'til after ten."

"Oh." I said. I felt like an idiot.

And just like that, my first semi-major event was over. I said good-bye to Chet and Bob and the other guy and left the bar.

Like so many other things, it had turned out to be a huge disappointment. Probably more so because of my truly *infantile*[11] expectations.

But the second major event didn't disappoint. In fact, the second major event, which was really a series of major events, proved to be completely memorable and monumental. So much so that I believe it deserves its own section. I truly hope you have prepared yourself for what happened to me next.

---

[11]**in•fan•tile** [**in**-f*uh*n-tahyl] *adj.* 1. relating to infants or infancy 2. suitable to or characteristic of infancy, especially regarding extreme immaturity

See jejune.

PART II

slings
and
arrows

once upon a time
there was
chapter eight

The most terrible part of my story, as I said, was really a chain of events. They started innocently enough with a notice on a bulletin board.

I had made it through two-thirds of the school year, and I had managed to make it through alive. True, I was tortured in a variety of ways on a semi-daily basis, but as I said before, there were a lot of good things that happened, too.

My parents were happy because my grades were actually pretty good. It turns out that Loyola had managed to deliver in one respect: it was a pretty good school for learning.

I found my classes challenging, with maybe the exception of American History. Poor Coach Collier was such a rotten teacher that most of us found his class to be a real joke. He was the type of teacher who never knew what the hell he was doing and was always looking to his students to remind him what chapter we were on or what he had assigned from last class.

I could almost believe that he was playing dumb deliberately and that he used this as a tool to constantly test us on whether we knew what was right or not. He'd be in the middle of a lecture on, say, the Enlightenment, and confuse Newton with Galileo and John Locke with Jean-Jacques Rousseau.

And his spelling was *deplorable*[12].

Actual notes from the board:

Missisippi River – lifeline to the fronteir

Great Britian – Seven Years War

French and Indian allyes pilage settlments

The only thing that saved this class from being a total waste of time was that Coach Collier figured out really early on that I knew how to spell, that I read the assignments, and that I kept up with the curriculum. I became a kind of student assistant for him. He sat me right up in the front, and when he was writing on the board if he was about to misspell a word I'd cough and then murmur the correct spelling for him. When he was about to start class, he'd look over at me for a correct chapter or page number. And when he was lecturing, if his facts started to veer off track I'd clear my throat and he would turn whatever he was saying into a question, then call on me or someone else in the class to get it straight.

Fritz was absolutely right about Brother Clive. As long as you let him fondle you, you could get away with murder in his class. I was pulling an A+ in the class and I know I turned in at least three labs late and one I never turned in at all. And all

---

[12]**de•plor•a•ble** [di-**plawr**-*uh*-b*uh*l] *adj.* 1. that which creates anguish or mourning, or the subject of distress 2. causing or deserving censure or contempt: *His financial records were in a deplorable state.*

I love this word. It applies to so many things and situations. Try it out, I think you'll like it.

it cost me was a couple of thigh squeezes, an occasional hair tousle, and one pat on my ass.

I think my second favorite class was turning out to be Religion. Brother Sullivan was such a nice man and it was clear that he was so passionate about what he was teaching. He told us all about how he had gotten the call to join the Jesuit order when he was fourteen. He had lived on a farm outside of a town called Guttenberg, which was near Dubuque. He told us that he was milking the cows one morning before school and he heard the voice of the Lord speak to him and tell him to join the order of the Jesuits in St. Louis. When he joined the order they sent him to Loyola University in Maryland and he learned to be a teacher.

The best thing about Brother Sullivan was that he didn't expect everyone to share his faith. In fact, he seemed to really enjoy engaging in debates with the students on religious doctrine and biblical stories. And the more we argued with him, the more he liked it. He told us that the foundation of faith was freedom of thought and freedom of choice and that a good scholar always adopted a healthy manner of *skepticism* [13] about anything that one was studying. And he told us that his job as a teacher was to instill in us a love of learning and a desire to question. He said that he could tell us what he believed, but that it was up to us to form our own opinions based on what we had read and studied. I thought that was pretty cool.

---

[13]**skep•ti•cis•m** [**skep**-t*uh*-siz-*uh*m] *n.* 1. an attitude of doubt or incredulity 2. the doctrine or philosophy that true belief is unattainable or should be suspended 3. uncertainty or disbelief regarding religious dogma

I used this word with Coach Collier once and he looked at me like I had sprouted a second head.

Brother Sullivan was also just a really great guy. Maybe because he was so young, he talked to us like equals, not like teacher and student. And his manner was so gentle and kind that you couldn't help but feel close to him. Just being around him made me want to be a kinder, more compassionate person.

But best of all was Brother Marvin's Creative Writing class. I looked forward to going there every day. Just being in the class made me feel like an adult, and most of the other students had accepted me as a part of the group. Dieter Schwarz would still criticize my writing every chance he got, but he had quickly figured out that Brother Marvin wasn't going to stand for any of his nasty bullshit, and had learned to frame his feedback in a way that was, if not considerate and constructive, at least relatively neutral.

And Brother Marvin had quickly become my favorite person in the whole school. His weird voice, coupled with his dry sense of humor, made every day in that class like watching an Oscar Wilde play.

One day he was talking to us about the use of metaphor in writing.

"A metaphor can be a very strong way to make a point to your reader," he said. "Unlike a simile, that makes a comparison between two things, a metaphor actively states that one thing actually is another; as in: 'Amanda, your hair is spun gold' or 'Dieter, you are the Pied Piper of all girls.' But you need to be aware of relying too heavily on clichés when you write. It is very easy to start your story with 'It was a dark and stormy night' or use the phrase 'it was raining cats and dogs.' Think about the flexibility of the English language and take the time to shape your words so that they say exactly what you want them to say. You might start a story with something like: 'The night was a bubbling cauldron of

bile and terror' or you might say that 'the steady downpour of rain was God pissing all over my dreams.'"

Brother Marvin always had a kind word for me, and he seemed to genuinely like my writing. I had presented another story to the class about a boy who finds the entrance to another world through the loose floorboards under his bed. Brother Marvin told me I should submit the story to the school's literary magazine which would be compiled and published by the Creative Writing class at the end of the year.

So even though I got called a lot of names and I wasn't very popular, there was a lot of really great stuff happening. Then I saw the notice on the bulletin board.

In the main hallway on the first floor was a large bulletin board where teachers and school organizations posted all kinds of notices. Because I spent so much time waiting around after school, I had become intimately familiar with everything on this board. I checked it every day and was always up on the latest posting.

Since my humiliating *foray*[14] into the not-so-sleazy underworld of gay nightlife, I had returned to waiting for my mom to pick me up after school. My mom had even told me that I could take the bus home from now on if I wanted to, but I told her that the bus that picked up the students in front of the school was such a cesspool that I would rather wait for her to give me a ride, if it was all the same to her. While it

---

[14]**for•ay** [**fawr**-ey, **for**-ey] *n.* 1. a raid or quick invasion 2. a sudden invasion, especially for war or spoils 3. a first attempt or brief excursion, especially outside of one's own confort zone

   I just pictured myself going into Auntie Dick's dressed as a Viking.

was true that Auntie Dick's turned out to be about as sleazy or underworld-y as an episode of *Leave it to Beaver*, it was still a humiliating experience and a huge disappointment. And I didn't want to have to be reminded of my innocent little field trip every single day for the rest of the school year. Mom and I luckily agreed that she would keep picking me up after school, at least for the time being. And we could revisit the subject in a couple of months.

So in the first week of March I found myself standing in the main hallway after school, staring at this notice on the bulletin board:

The Drama Club
at
St. Ignatius Loyola

will be holding AUDITIONS
for the Spring Production of

HAMLET

Those interested in auditioning
should sign up with Ms. Vasquez in
Room 221 by Monday, March 10

I studied the posting very carefully for several minutes.

Ms. Vasquez, I knew, was a brand new lay teacher at the school. She had replaced Brother Schafer, who had taught at SILHS for over forty years and had finally retired and returned to his hometown of Tuscaloosa, Alabama. He had taught upper level English.

I had only seen her a couple of times. She was pretty young, probably in her early thirties, and very compact. She couldn't have been any more than 5'1" or 5'2" and she had a beautiful caramel-colored complexion. She wore her hair in a short pixie style and her body was tight and athletic, like a runner. And she wore slacks. When she joined the school she became the only female teacher on the faculty.

I thought it was pretty interesting that such a new teacher would be taking on a project like this. But even more than that, I was fascinated and frightened by the idea of auditioning for a play. And the play itself was intimidating. I mean, *Hamlet* was probably the greatest play in the English language. I had read some Shakespeare, but I hadn't been in any kind of a performance since I played one of the Three Wise Men in a Christmas pageant at my old elementary school. And that could hardly be called acting, since all I did was walk onto the stage wearing a silk caftan that belonged to my mother and a crown I had made out of cardboard and aluminum foil. I carried a gold box and placed it in front of a manger that held a plastic baby doll as Jesus Christ. I mean, I didn't even have any lines.

The idea rolled around constantly in my head over the next day and a half. I finally decided to bring the idea to my committee of oddball friends.

The five of us sat at our regular table in the corner of the cafeteria during lunchtime on Wednesday. We were exchanging the usual chitchat about school and classes and all that other boring stuff.

"Hey, Stuart," Jacob said. "Did you turn in that lab on genetics that was due for Brother Clive?"

"Not yet. I let Brother Clive pinch my cheek, tho that should buy me at leatht another week."

"These tater tots taste like my ass," said Nels.

"How would you know?" asked Fritz.

"Your mom told me," said Nels.

"Have any of you guys met Ms. Vasquez?" I asked casually.

"I met her," said Stuart. "She thtopped that athhole Taylor from mething with me in the hall jutht yethterday. She theems pretty cool."

"I think she looks like a dyke," said Nels.

"That's a pretty shitty thing to say," I snapped.

"Sah-ree, psycho." Nels replied, sarcastically. "I didn't realize the two of you were dating."

"I just don't think you should be saying something nasty like that, especially about someone you don't even know."

"Since when did you become such a teachers' rights activist?" Nels shot back.

"All right, all right, calm down you two." Fritz said. "Why do you ask about Ms. Vasquez, Charles?"

"I saw a notice about auditioning for the spring production of *Hamlet*." I said. "I was thinking I might give it a shot."

"Theriouthly?" said Stuart. "I didn't know you were into acting."

"Well, I'm not, really. I just thought it looked like an interesting thing to do. But I don't even want to try out if she's in charge of the whole thing and she isn't a cool teacher to work with."

"What did the notice say?" asked Jacob.

"It just said if you were interested in auditioning you should see Ms. Vasquez."

"Well go by and ask her for more details," said Jacob.

"And when you find out more, let me know," said Nels. "I might be interested in auditioning, too."

"Me too," said Stuart.

That afternoon I went to room 221 as soon as the school day was over. The classroom was still emptying out and Ms. Vasquez was standing at her desk, collecting papers. I walked up to her desk and stood off to the side, waiting until she was free. She noticed me right away.

"Hi!" she said brightly. "Can I help you with something?"

"Um, I was wondering about the notice I saw on the bulletin board for auditions."

"Did you want to sign up?" she asked, smiling at me.

"I'm not really sure," I said. "I guess I'd be interested in hearing a little more about it."

"Well, let's see. The auditions will be held next week. And then the rehearsals start the week after that. The show is scheduled to open the second week of May and will run for two weekends."

"Do I need to have any experience?" I asked, shyly.

"No, not at all," she said, punching me lightly on the shoulder. "We'll take anybody. You never know who might be the next Laurence Olivier." She smiled warmly at me again.

"How often are the rehearsals?" I asked.

"Monday through Friday from three to six. It is Shakespeare, but we'll be working from a script that has been edited down significantly. How are your grades?"

"My grades are great," I said.

"Because you need to be passing all your subjects, and you can't allow your grades to slip during rehearsals. Your schoolwork has to come first. Can I put you down for an audition time?"

"I'm not sure yet. I mean, I don't really even know if I would be any good."

"Well, how about this? Take these excerpts from the script and look them over." She handed me a Xeroxed piece of paper. "These are what we'll be using in the auditions. But you'll need to sign up by Friday if you plan to audition. Think it over and come back and see me if you want to give it a shot. What do you say, um . . . I didn't get your name."

"Charles. Charles Siskin."

"Okay, Charles Charles Siskin. Think it over and come back to see me." She smiled at me again and then turned to another student who was waiting to speak to her.

I reported everything back to the gang at lunch the next day.

"Tho, are you going to try out?" asked Stuart.

"I don't know. Do you think I should?" I took in the whole group when I asked this question.

"Why not?" Nels said. "I mean, what's the worst that could happen? They probably won't cast any freshmen in any big roles anyway. I'm going to try out."

"You are?" I said.

"Sure. I mean even if I don't get a part, there's bound to be something I can do like with sets or sound or something. I think it'll be a great way to meet new people."

"You mean girls, don't you?" said Fritz.

"There'll be girls in the play?" asked Jacob.

"Of course there'll be girls," said Fritz. "Who do you think are going to play the girls' parts? St. Lo boys in wigs and dresses?"

"That'th how they did it in Shakethpeare'th time," said Stuart.

"My English teacher told me they do a show every year," said Fritz, "and they always use girls from St. Cecilia's for the female roles."

"Well, that seals the deal for me," said Nels. "I need to get a date before the end of my freshman year or my balls are going to fall off from lack of use."

"If they don't fall off from masturbation first," said Fritz.

"If that could happen, none of us would have any balls," said Jacob.

"You guyth are dithguthting," said Stuart.

"Alright, so who's in?" said Nels.

"I'd shit my pants if I had to get up on a stage," said Jacob.

"Forget it," said Fritz. "I'm not dropping Chess Club for anything."

"We can pull out of Cheth Club and then go back after," said Stuart.

"Geek," said Nels.

"Jackass," said Fritz.

"Let'th do it," said Stuart.

"Are you in, Charles?" asked Nels.

"Yeah. I guess I am."

"Great!" Nels said. "Let's meet up at Ms. Vasquez's room after school today."

So Nels, Stuart, and I met up at Ms. Vasquez's room right after school. She greeted us as warmly as she had greeted me the day before. She gave each of them the same page of Shakespearean text she had given me.

"So just select a piece of dialogue from the play that you like and prepare to read it for the audition," she said. "Now I can't stress this enough. You don't have to memorize it. In fact, I would prefer that you didn't. I'd like you to focus more on how you deliver the lines. I'll be looking for how well you understand the language and how well you can communicate the meaning as you read." She showed us a sign-up list with time slots of ten minutes each. "Here you go, boys. Auditions are Monday and Tuesday after school, starting at three, but I'm afraid Monday is already filled up. Just pick a time slot and sign away."

Nels signed up for three-forty, Stuart for four o'clock. The only time slot left was five-fifty. I could tell my mom to pick me up a little later than usual.

I studied the excerpts on the page for two days before finally selecting one. It read like this:

> HAMLET: What a piece of work is man! How noble in reason! how infinite in faculties! In form and moving how express and admirable! In action how like an Angel! In apprehension how like a god! The beauty of the world! The paragon of animals! And yet to me, what is this quintessence of dust? Man delights not me; no, nor Woman neither; though by your smiling you seem to say so.

I couldn't believe that writing like that was possible. I mean, I knew Shakespeare was a genius and all, but I couldn't believe how well he had summed up how I felt about the world and the people and things in it. In just a few sentences he had captured the ambivalence I felt about the people and the world around me. I had definitely found the speech I wanted to use for my audition.

I studied the speech all weekend and by Tuesday afternoon I felt like I really had it nailed down. I had also managed to work myself up into a true panic.

In the afternoon, I went up to Ms. Vasquez's room and sat outside on the floor in the hall. I had almost three hours to wait until my time to audition came up. At three-thirty Nels and Stuart showed up together. We all sat on the floor in the hall, waiting to be called.

"I swear to God I'm going to puke," Nels said. "Why would anyone do this? This is horrible."

"Jethuth, what a baby," said Stuart. "I mean, what'th the wortht that could happen? You go in, you thay your little thpeech and in the middle of your audition you crap yourthelf like a two year old."

"Bite my bag," said Nels. We sat for several minutes in silence. Nels was called in at precisely three-forty and came out seven minutes later.

"A piece of cake," he said. "I told you there was nothing to worry about."

"What happened?" I asked.

"Nothing. I went in, she asked me a few questions, I read the lines, she asked me to read them again and that was it."

"What did she athk you?" Stuart said.

"I don't know. She asked me what grade I was in and what kinds of things I liked to do when I wasn't in school. Junk like that. She's really nice."

"How do you think you did?" I asked.

"Hell, who knows? She said there would be callback auditions tomorrow and that the cast list would be posted by Friday. Listen, punks. I have to go. I'll see you tomorrow at lunch." Nels left Stuart and me sitting in the hallway.

Several other students I recognized but didn't know came and went for their auditions. At three fifty-eight Stuart was called in. He came out eight minutes later.

"Theriouthly, Charleth. I think I'm in love."

"What?"

"Mth. Vathqueth ith a total babe. And she'th tho nithe!"

"What happened?" By this time, my whole body was sweating profusely.

"It wath jutht like Nelth thaid. She athked me a couple of questionth, I read my lineth and then she athked me to read them again. Oh, she told me to thlow down and to pay clothe attenthion to the punctuation."

I breathed a little easier, but my palms were still sweating and my heart was still beating a little faster than usual. I let out a huge sigh and settled my back against the wall.

"Tho, do you want me to wait with you until you go in?" Stuart asked. It was pretty clear he was ready to go home.

"No, that's crazy." I said. "It's almost two hours. Go on home and I'll see you in the morning."

"All right, if you're sure," he said, already moving down the hall. "I'll thee you tomorrow in the cafeteria before thchool." He walked farther down the hall then looked back over his shoulder. "Oh, good luck!" he yelled, and then disappeared down the stairs.

I sat and looked at my lines one more time and waited.

As it was getting close to five o'clock, I heard a voice from down the hall on my right.

"Well. If it isn't little Charlie Sissykins." It was Dieter Schwarz. I turned away and tried to pretend he wasn't there. "What's wrong, Sissykins? Are you lost?" I looked up at him as he stood over me.

"I'm waiting to audition for the play," I said, then pretended to study my lines. Dieter burst out laughing.

"You? So you're not only a prize-winning author, but an actor, too? Is there no end to your talent?" He sneered down at me, then kicked the paper out of my hand with one shiny, steel-toed boot.

"Why don't you go salute yourself," I said, reaching across the floor for my page of lines.

"How about this," he said, stepping on my hand as I reached out to grab the page.

"Ow! Get off my hand, you Nazi."

"Why don't you sit your ass right there," he sneered, "and you can salute me when I get cast in the lead role." He released my hand from under his boot.

"You seem pretty sure of yourself," I said, rubbing my hand.

"I've had the lead two years running. Why should this year be any different?" he said scornfully.

"Brother Schafer's not here anymore," I said. "Maybe Ms. Vasquez won't want a marching penis as the lead in her show." I couldn't believe that those words had just come out of my mouth.

Before I could even blink, Dieter had leaned over and picked me up from the floor by the front of my shirt. "What did you say to me?"

At that moment, the classroom door opened and Ms. Vasquez poked her head out. Dieter released me immediately and I stumbled back against the wall. She looked quizzically at us both for a moment.

"Dieter Schwarz?" she said.

"Yes ma'am, that's me," he said, without missing a beat.

"C'mon in, Dieter. You're next." He pushed past me without so much as a glance in my direction.

Seven and a half minutes later he came out again and walked away without a word or a look in my direction.

At five-fifty sharp, the door opened and Ms. Vasquez leaned out.

"Well, champ. It looks like you're the last one. Come on in."

I walked into the empty classroom. Ms. Vasquez sat down at a desk facing a space she had cleared at the front of the room.

"So, Charles. I'm really glad to see you decided to audition. I know it takes a lot of guts to try this kind of thing. Is this your first year at Loyola?"

"Yes, ma'am." I said shakily.

"Oh, please . . . no ma'am's, okay? It makes me feel like I'm eighty years old."

"Yes, ma'am. I mean. Yes. Ms. Vasquez."

"Listen, Charlie. You're going to need to relax. You're going to pass out if you don't calm down. Now, tell me a little about yourself. What kinds of things do you like to do?"

"Well. I read a lot. And I like to write."

"Really? What are you reading right now?"

"I'm reading a collection of short stories by Shirley Jackson, *The World According to Garp* by John Irving, and I just started *Look Homeward, Angel* by Thomas Wolfe."

"Wow. You're reading all of that at the same time?"

I think I blushed a little. "Yeah. I generally read two or three books at a time. That way I can pick up whichever one suits my mood at the time."

"I see. And what excerpt have you chosen for the audition today?"

"I chose 'What a piece of work is man.'"

"Okay, shoot." She wrote something down on the notebook in front of her and then looked up at me.

I read the lines, careful not to read too fast. When I was done, I looked at her and held my breath.

"Okay. That was great. Now, tell me something. Why did you choose that piece?"

I thought for a moment. "Well, it really spoke to me," I finally said. "I felt like Shakespeare had looked right into my head and put my feelings on paper. It was really weird."

"So what do you think Hamlet means when he's saying these lines?"

"Well, I think he's saying that he feels two ways about people. That a person is a really amazing thing, or at least could be. But it seems like Hamlet is disappointed. Not just in people, but because he can't seem to find the joy in things. That there are these amazing things around him called man, but he can't seem to take pleasure or see the good in them. And I think he's a little jealous of the person he's talking to, because that person seems to be able to enjoy life a lot more than he does."

"And you identify with those thoughts?" She looked me closely in the eyes.

"Yeah. I really do. And it makes me kind of disappointed in myself that I don't see more value in the beauty that's around me."

"Think about all those things you just said, and speak the lines again."

I took a breath and before I began I started thinking about all the things that had happened to me over the past years. I thought of Dieter's boot on my hand and the word "queer" written on my locker. Then I thought about Phaedre and Stuart and Sammy and even Chet and Bob and the other guy in Auntie Dick's whose name I never found out. I thought about my mother and my father and even that substitute teacher I had in the first grade. And I found that I could say the lines without looking at the paper. And when I came to the part that said "Man delights not me" I thought about all the kids who had called me names and J.J. Barker who had punched me in the stomach for dancing with a bunch of girls. I thought about Alejandro Taylor and my first day at Loyola. I paused for a moment, afraid that if I spoke another word I would burst out crying like a little baby. I took a hitching breath and swallowed hard and then looked down at the floor. My hand was clutching at my leg so hard I could feel my nails digging into my flesh. Then I said the words. And then I lifted my head and looked Ms. Vasquez in the eyes and said: "Though by your smiling you seem to say so."

We looked at each other in silence for a moment, then she stood up and walked over to me.

"Thank you, Charles," she said. "That was lovely." She put her hand on my shoulder. "I'll post a callback list outside my room tomorrow morning for any students whom I need to see more from. Then the cast list will go up on Friday afternoon."

I turned and left the room.

The next morning I met up with Stuart and Nels in the cafeteria.

"Have you seen the callback list yet?" Nels asked.

"No," I said. "I just got here. Why don't we go up now?" The three of us left the cafeteria and climbed the stairs to the second floor.

The list was posted on the wall outside Ms. Vasquez's room, and several students were gathered around it.

"Go check the list, Charles." Nels said to me. "I'm too nervous." The few people gathered around the list had started to move away and I approached it, my heart beating quickly. I scanned the list quickly. There were about twenty names on the list:

"Saul Friedman, David Garcia, Nels Horst . . . " One down. "Amanda Rice, Joel Sanders, Stuart Simpson, Anna Trujillo, Joe York . . . " My name wasn't on the callback list. I didn't even make it past the first cut. I walked slowly over to Nels and Stuart. "You both got called back." I said and then started down the hall.

"Wait a thec!" Stuart said. "Weren't you on the litht?"

"No," I said. "I guess acting isn't my thing."

It kind of sucked, but I wasn't going to let it get me down. I mean, what did I expect? That I would get called back and then get cast in the show with absolutely no experience? But Nels and Stuart didn't have any experience and they got called back. And Stuart had a lisp as thick as my arm! Whatever. I wasn't going to obsess about it. There were a lot of other things I could do besides being in some stupid play. And to Stuart and Nels's credit, neither one of them mentioned the callbacks for the next two days.

I was standing at my locker on Friday afternoon when Nels came running down the hall at me.

"Did you see the cast list!" He said, breathlessly.

"No." I said. "I was just going to head downstairs and wait for my mom. Why, did you get cast?"

"Yeah! Stuart and I both got cast. He's playing someone named Rosencrantz and I'm playing someone named Guildenstern. But that's not what I'm talking about. You haven't seen the list?"

"No," I said, slightly irritated. "What's the point? I didn't even make it to the callbacks."

"C'mon. You need to check the list." He grabbed me by the arm and pulled me down the hall.

"All right! All right! Let go of me!" He pushed me ahead of him down the hall and to the stairway.

On the second floor there were still several people milling around in the hall outside of Ms. Vasquez's room. Stuart was standing off to one side.

I walked up to the list posted on the wall.

"Hamlet," it said, "dot, dot, dot . . . Charles Siskin."

I stared at the list for what seemed like an hour. How could this be?

"Charleth, can you believe it?" Stuart said. "My betht friend ith the lead in the thpring play!" He and Nels clapped me on the shoulders. "And you jutht mithed it. Dieter Schwarz came down and thaw that he wath playing Claudiuth and thaid 'you can tell that thtupid bitch that if she thinkth I'm playing anything leth than the lead, she'th fucking crathy! You can tell her not to exthpect me at rehearthalth!' then he thtormed off like a little girl."

Nels and Stuart laughed out loud, but I just kept looking at the list. I just couldn't believe it.

"Come on," said Nels. "Let's walk down to the Seven Eleven and get some sodas to celebrate. My treat."

"You guys go on," I said. "I need to talk to Ms. Vasquez."

"Theriouthly? He getth hith firtht big part and already he'th too big to athothiate with the little people."

"Come on Stuart," said Nels, with mock hurt and disdain. "Who needs that prima donna? We can enjoy our sodas all by ourselves." They turned away in phony disgust and stomped down the hallway.

"Have a great weekend," yelled Stuart, over his shoulder, "and thee you at rehearthal."

I looked at the list one more time, than went into Ms. Vasquez's room. She was sitting at her desk grading papers. When I entered the room she looked up and a smile spread across her face.

"Ms. Vasquez? May I speak with you?" She immediately looked concerned.

"Is everything okay, Charles?"

"Yes, ma'am. I mean, yes . . . I think so. I just don't understand."

"Understand what, sweetie?"

"I don't understand how I got that part. I mean, I didn't even get asked to the callbacks."

"I didn't need to ask you to the callbacks, sweetie. I knew you'd be my Hamlet as soon as you left that first day."

"But how? I mean how can you be sure?"

"Well, I guess I can't be totally sure." She stood up and came around the desk and sat on the edge. "But I've directed a play or two in my time, and I usually have pretty good instincts about casting. They say 90% of the director's talent is in the right casting. And I guess I saw something in you. A depth of feeling that is lacking in a lot of young actors. I look into your eyes and I see an old soul there. A gravity and a weariness that kind of breaks my heart. And those are the qualities I want for my Hamlet."

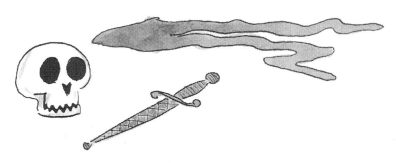

HAMLET SUPPLIES

there once was a chapter named nine

"I can't believe it," said Phaedre in Creative Writing class on Monday. "I don't think there's ever been a freshman cast in a lead role in the spring play. At least not since I've been going to school here."

Dieter wasn't even in school today. At least he wasn't in class.

"Of course he isn't," said Phaedre. "What a pussy. What did your parents say?"

"Well, they were totally thrilled, of course," I said. "My mom cried a little and my dad gave me a slap on the back. And you remember me telling you about Sammy? She almost broke the phone shrieking when I called and told her."

"Phaedre? Charles? You're supposed to be trading writing assignments, not gossiping like two fishwives."

"Sorry, Brother Marvin." Fishwives?

Phaedre lowered her voice and leaned over her paper, gesturing to it constantly while she talked so it looked like we were talking about the writing assignment.

"So when do you start rehearsals?" she asked.

"Today!" I said. "I'm so excited I feel like I'm going to piss myself."

"Well, I think that's fantastic." She pointed to her paper for extra emphasis. "I'm sure you're going to be great, and I can't wait for opening night."

"Oh, God. I think I'm going to puke." I said.

"You'll be fine," she whispered. "Vasquez wouldn't have

picked you if she didn't think you could do it. I just wish I could have been there when Herr Schwarz found out he didn't get the lead. With my camera."

"I'm actually really glad he isn't here today. I'm pretty sure he's going to kill me when he sees me."

"Let him try. I'll cut his balls off and serve them to him for breakfast."

"Mr. Siskin? Miss Brodowski? Final warning." Brother Marvin was standing right over us. We hadn't even heard him walk up.

"Yes, Brother."

That afternoon I made my way to Ms. Vasquez's room as soon as my last class was over. Ms. Vasquez's room was completely empty when I got there. Like a total geek I sat in the front row of the classroom and took out my brand new paperback copy of *Hamlet* (purchased this past weekend at Walden's Books), two pens (one blue, one red), two sharpened pencils, a highlighter, and a new binder that I found at Walgreen's that now had a Xeroxed copy of a picture of William Shakespeare taped to the front that I nabbed at the library before school started.

I was already about halfway through reading the play. The paperback edition that I got had *copious*[15] footnotes on each facing page of the script that helped me decipher the language. I was really hoping that this edited version that we would be doing was really edited, because from what I had read so far, Hamlet had an assload of lines.

---

[15]**co•pi•ous** [**koh**-pee-*uh*s] *adj.* 1. yielding something plentifully 2. full of information or thought 3. on a large scale or in large amounts

Here's a word that can really get you punched in the nuts if you try to use it in everyday language.

But even as I worried about the sheer volume of line memorization I would have to undertake, I couldn't help wishing at the same time that I would be allowed to speak all of these amazing words. I mean, how great is this:

How weary, stale, flat and unprofitable
Seem to me all the uses of the world.

I was going to have the chance to say these words, to speak them as if they were my own, on a stage in front of who knows how many people.

I sat waiting patiently for the first cast members to arrive. Thank God Stuart and Nels were the first ones there.

"Really, *Schmendrick*[16]? You have to thit in the front row?" said Stuart as he took the seat behind me. Nels sat one seat back and to my left.

"Hey shut up, Stu. He's Hamlet, for Christ's sake. He's the freaking Prince of Denmark."

"Thomeone'th been thtudying up," said Stuart, throwing an eraser at Nels's head.

"Bite my bag," said Nels.

A few more boys came into the room. Our school was so small that I recognized all the faces, but didn't yet know any of them by name. They scattered around the room and sat down, looking us over suspiciously.

---

[16]**Schmendrick** [**shmen**-drik] *n.* 1. A stupid and ineffectual nobody. From Yiddish shmendrik, the name of a character in an operetta by Avrom Goldfaden (1840-1908), Father of Yiddish Theater. 2. a guy who thinks that money, fashion sense, and the proper affectation equals coolness. A poser.

This is not a vocabulary word, it's just a word that Stuart uses all the time. But I thought you might appreciate an explanation, nonetheless.

A few minutes later Amanda Rice, a girl from my Creative Writing class, came in. She came right up to me and stuck out her hand. "Charles!" she said, brightly. "It looks like I'll be playing your mother!" I shook her hand, not knowing what else to do.

"Um . . . hi, Mom." I said. She giggled loudly and then swept past me and found a seat toward the back of the room.

More boys came in, including one boy who had caught me staring at him on more than one occasion. I was pretty sure his name was Alex something. He was a sophomore, a little taller than I was with jet-black curly hair, ice-blue eyes and skin the color of fresh cream. I looked away from him as soon as he met my eyes.

Just then Ms. Vasquez came in the room, followed by a junior whose name I didn't know.

"Okay, if everybody can find a seat, we can get started." I looked at the clock. It was precisely three. Way to go, Ms. Vasquez! (I'm a sucker for punctuality.)

"First, let me introduce you to Clark Rudnick. He's going to be our stage manager. Clark, will you pass the scripts out to everybody?" He picked up a stack of neatly bound scripts that sat on the edge of Ms. Vasquez's desk and began to pass them out. "As soon as everyone has a script, Clark will take the roll and we can begin. You should probably know that Clark is going to be my right-hand man. Every day that you're called to rehearse, you need to check in with Clark so that he knows that you're here. And just to be clear, I am strict about time. I will do my best not to waste your time, and I expect that you will do your best not to waste mine."

Clark finished passing out the scripts and then proceeded to call the roll. "Dieter Schwarz as Claudius." There was a silence as everyone looked around the room. "Dieter Schwarz?" he said again. Several people looked at the ground.

"Does anyone know where Dieter Schwarz is?" Ms. Vasquez asked. There was a heavy silence. Finally a boy near me raised his hand.

"I'm pretty sure Dieter has withdrawn from the show," the boy said.

"And you say this because . . . ?" Ms. Vasquez asked.

"Well," the boy said, staring hard at the ground, "he told me he wouldn't be caught dead playing any other part but Hamlet," the boy said.

"I see," said Ms. Vasquez. "Well, that's too bad for him. I'm glad to see that no one else here is that petty and small-minded." She frowned and looked at her nails, then signaled for Clark to continue.

"Charles Siskin as Hamlet," he said. There was a faint buzz in the class followed by a smattering of applause. I felt myself turning bright red as everyone in the room looked at me. Ms. Vasquez smiled and nodded to Clark.

"Anton Kovac as Polonius?" called Clark.

"Here." It was the boy who had offered the news about Dieter. He continued calling out the names of the cast members.

"Alex Davidson as Laertes?" It was the boy who had caught me staring at him more than once. The boy with the black curly hair and the ice-blue eyes. He looked over toward me, but didn't seem to see me.

"Ezra Gold as Horatio? Stuart Simpson as Rosencrantz? Nels Horst as Guildenstern? Amanda Rice as Gertrude? Patricia Jackson as Ophelia?" I looked over to see who would respond as the actor playing my love interest. A pretty, quiet girl I hadn't even seen come in the room raised her hand and replied "here" in a voice that was barely audible. She had huge brown eyes and skin that was the color of dark walnut wood, warm and deep and gleaming. She was absolutely stunning, but her manner was so withdrawn and timid that it seemed that she might burst into tears at any moment.

Clark continued with the roll call. Most of the other actors were playing several parts, assorted gentlemen and a priest, servants, the players, and the ghost of Hamlet's father. Once Clark had finished the roll and we could see that everyone except Dieter was here, Ms. Vasquez addressed the cast.

"Well, here we all are. Once I've had the chance to speak to Dieter I will recast the role of Claudius. In the meantime, a few things you should know about me. I have some of you as my students but most of you don't know me at all, since I'm relatively new here. My degree is in English with a minor in theatre, and I've acted in and directed many plays.

"I believe that the best theatrical work is done collaboratively, so I expect everyone to contribute their ideas, their thoughts and so forth, with the understanding that as the director I have the final say in all decisions regarding the final look and feel of the play. Just like sailing a ship, a play requires a strong sense of leadership so that the final product can be cohesive.

"I've already told you that Clark is my right-hand man, and I expect you to treat him as such. Any instructions he might give you will be coming from me and I expect you all to respect that. This isn't a teacher--student kind of thing but the way that a professional production is run. I will run this production as much like a professional production as I can, and I have very high expectations for all of you.

"Now, enough of my flapping my lips. Let's read through the play. The script you have is significantly edited down from the original. I don't expect any Oscar-winning performances today, so let's just relax, read through and if you have any questions, let me know. I'll read the stage directions and Clark, if you wouldn't mind reading Claudius for today?"

With that, we all opened our scripts and began to read.

"The read-through was amazing!" I said to my mother on the way home. "Everyone was so perfect for their parts and the more we read the more excited I got. I think this is going to be a fantastic play!"

"Well, that's wonderful," my mother said. "And of course now you'll have plenty to keep you busy while you're waiting for me to come pick you up after school."

"And since we don't finish rehearsal until six, you don't have to rush to pick me up."

As we drove down the highway, I looked out the window at the road and the trees and the buildings rushing past. For once everything seemed to be going right. Maybe things were going to be okay after all.

I opened my script and began to study my lines, smiling quietly to myself.

the legend of
chapter ten

Dieter returned to Creative Writing class the next day. For once he wasn't wearing his uniform, but it just so happened that I was. I had no idea if Ms. Vasquez had spoken to him or not, but he came right up to me before class started. Brother Marvin was just outside the classroom in the hall and Phaedre hadn't arrived yet.

"I just wanted to congratulate you," he said, looking down his nose at me. "I'm sure you're going to make a fine Hamlet. If your acting sucks dick as much as you do, the audience will probably demand their money back." He put one hand into the brown sack lunch he was carrying and withdrew a chocolate pudding cup. Crushing the cup with one hand, he smeared the pudding down the front of my uniform shirt, then smeared a stripe of chocolate down one of my cheeks and up the other. He walked away, wiping his hand on a paper towel he took out of his book satchel.

I sat there for a moment, not believing what had just happened. There were only a few other students in the classroom, but they were as shocked as I was. After only a moment, I burst out laughing. I mean, it was just so funny! I couldn't believe that big, strong, manly Dieter was acting like such a baby over a part in a play.

And no matter what he did, he still wouldn't be playing Hamlet. Even if he killed me I was pretty sure Ms. Vasquez would find someone else to play the part.

It just struck me as so fucking funny that I couldn't help

myself. I laughed out loud, long and hard. Phaedre came in the room and saw the mess I was in.

"What happened to you?" she said, but I couldn't catch my breath, I was laughing so hard. I looked over at Dieter and his face was purple with rage. He sat at his desk, his hands clenching into fists and unclenching over and over again.

I walked to the door of the classroom and went out into the hall where Brother Marvin was standing.

"Brother, may I be excused?" I was barely able to gasp out between gales of laughter. I didn't even wait for a response and went straight to the restroom to clean myself up.

The uniform was a total loss for the day, but I explained to Colonel Frack that I had had an accident with my lunch and he let it slide.

After an endless conference in Brother Baker's office it was finally decided that Dieter would get a single day of in-school suspension, mostly because I refused to rat him out and no one else in the class really saw exactly what happened. I could see that it frustrated the hell out of Brother Baker that he couldn't suspend Dieter for three days like he wanted to, but I wasn't about to add squealing on him to my list of crimes against Herr Schwarz.

And somehow the only thing I could really feel for him was sorry. Sorry that he was so immature and even a little sorry that I had taken away a part that had clearly meant so much to him. And I think that refusing to snitch on him actually stopped him from doing me serious bodily harm because after that he just kind of stayed away from me.

As the days went by I began to live for two things: Creative Writing class and play rehearsal.

I was learning so much in Creative Writing that it was unbelievable. I don't think I have ever been aware of actually making progress as much as I was in writing. And it wasn't just because I was able to do a lot of writing. Every class and every week I got to hear the writing of the other students in the class. Even though it was a pretty small class (fifteen students plus me), there was a huge range in styles, subject matter and ability. And as I got to hear others' writing and offer feedback, I started to learn how to look at my own writing with an *objective*[17] eye. I began to examine my writing for strengths and weaknesses and I actually started to rewrite, which was something I had never done before.

As for the play, there was nothing better in the whole world than rehearsing. Nels and Stuart and I actually made some new friends from the cast—people who would even say hello to us in the halls.

And Ms. Vasquez was a genius.

She almost always knew the answer when I had a question about the lines. And unlike almost any other teacher I had ever had, if she didn't know the answer to something, she'd say "I don't know"! Then she'd usually find the answer or show us where we could find it ourselves.

And when she had talked about theatre being a collaborative art form, she meant it.

---

[17]**ob•jec•tive** [*uh*b-**jek**-tive] *adj.* 1. existing in reality separate from the mind 2. dealing with words that follow prepositions or transitive verbs 3. communicating or approaching facts or conditions as observed without altering them because of personal feelings or interpretation

This story is *not* objective. Everything I'm telling you about is from my point of view. For all you know, I could be totally screwed up and rewrote every event so that I came out looking like a star.

During rehearsal, while we'd be working on a scene, if somebody had a suggestion about something she almost always said "let's try it out and see what happens." And if it worked out well it became part of the play and if it didn't she was honest without being a bitch about it. She'd just say "I don't think that works. What else can we try?" So that it really felt like we were all working on the play together.

As rehearsals went on, I began to form a stronger and stronger bond with her. I would often stay after rehearsal was over and help her put her room back in order, put all the chairs back into their rows and such. We also spent a chunk of rehearsal time, just her and me, working on Hamlet's *soliloquies*[18]. And during these moments we had together, when no one else was around, we had some really great conversations.

One afternoon, about two weeks into rehearsals, we were spending the last part of the rehearsal day working on the famous "To be or not to be" speech.

"What is this speech about?" she asked. I stared hard at the script for a full minute. Finally, she said, "Let's start with the first line, To be or not to be: that is the question. What do you think that line means?"

"I'm not really sure," I said.

"What if you replace the word 'be' with the word 'live?'" she asked.

---

[18]**so•lil•o•quy** [*suh*-lil-*uh*-kwee] *n.* 1. an extended speech, especially in a play, by a single character as if he/she is alone; a theatrical device often used in Shakespeare and other plays to reveal the character's innermost thoughts: *In Hamlet, Shakespeare uses the soliloquy to allow his central character to make many reflections out loud.* 2. the speech resulting from talking to oneself

In the play Hamlet, *Hamlet has to say a shitload of soliloquies.*

"To live or not to live: that is the question." I said.

Suddenly, it all seemed clear. "He's talking about suicide! He's trying to decide if he should kill himself or not!" I looked at the rest of the speech. "He's trying to figure out if it's better to stick around and put up with a bunch of crap and pain or to just let go and give in to the peace and relief of death. Is that right?"

"That'll do, for a start," she replied.

"Wow. That's some heavy shi—I mean stuff."

"Yeah. No shi—I mean stuff," she said. We both laughed.

After we had been working for a while, Ms. Vasquez said:

"You know what, Ham?" She called me Ham. "Let's call it quits for the day. I'm beat and I've got a pile of papers to grade and a meeting I have to go to tonight. Help me with the desks, would you?"

"What kind of meeting are you going to?" I asked as we began to move the desks back into place. I was always fascinated by what my teachers did when they weren't teaching.

"Oh, this stupid motorcycle club I never should have joined."

"You have a motorcycle?!"

"Yeah. I'd ride it to work if I didn't think someone would steal it from the parking lot."

"I can't believe that! You don't seem like the motorcycle-riding type to me."

"There's a lot you don't know about me, kid." It was true.

"Yeah? Like what?"

She paused a moment. "Maybe when you're older," she finally said.

"Oh, come on. I've told you all kinds of things about me," I said. I really had. She knew where I lived, what school I had gone to before, even most of why I ended up at Loyola. I told her all about getting teased and picked on and how I had hoped that things would be different here and how let down I was when that didn't happen. I didn't tell her everything, like my attraction to boys of the same sex.

"Tell me one thing about you that would really surprise me." I said.

"Well," she said, scratching her head. "I used to be a nun."

"What?!?!" I almost fell over the desk I was moving.

"Yeah. I used to be a nun, a Carmelite nun."

"You've got to be shitting me!"

"I shit you not. I was a postulant for six months and then a novitiate for two years and then took first vows. But I left the order after two more years, right before I was set to take my final vows."

"Why did you leave?" I asked, still trying to wrap my head around this new information.

"I'm not sure it's appropriate to tell you, Ham. I mean, it's really kind of personal."

"Oh," I said, the disappointment clearly showing in my voice. We continued to move the desks back into place in silence. After we finished with the desks, she sat down in one desk near me.

"All right," she sighed heavily. "I guess it's only fair that I open up to you, since you've been so willing to open up to me. But you have to promise that it won't leave this room."

"I promise," I said, crossing my heart. And I meant it completely. "I'll take it to the grave."

"It's not that I'm ashamed or anything. And I really couldn't care less if the administration or the faculty knows. But I don't want my personal life to be fodder for student gossip and innuendo. Understand?"

"I completely understand." Boy, did I.

"I left because I couldn't continue to deny the fact that I was a lesbian."

I stared at her with my mouth open.

"Don't tell me you didn't suspect," she said, chuckling at my obvious shock.

"Well, I guess maybe I suspected a little." I said. "But, wow."

"Do the other kids talk about it?" she asked.

There had definitely been some *conjecture*[19] about Ms. Vasquez's sexuality. But I think I had really dismissed it all as a lot of talk by oversexed boys who didn't know how to deal with a woman who was strong and assertive and who didn't wear frilly dresses all the time (or ever).

"Yeah, I guess so. But I didn't really pay it that much mind. I mean it certainly didn't matter to me."

---

[19]**con•jec•ture** [k*uh*n-**jek**-cher] *n.* 1. *Obsolete.* Interpretation of omens; supposition 2. to infer a conclusion by guesswork 3. a proposition, as in mathematics, that has been neither proved nor disproved

It really pissed me off that everyone assumed I was gay when really it was only conjecture on their part.

"Well that's good to know," she said, looking at me intently. "I'd hate to think something as trivial as that would interfere with our relationship. I guess I wouldn't have told you if I thought it would. And I guess you know I think you're a pretty great kid." She smiled at me and patted my cheek.

"Ms. Vasquez?" I said.

"Yeah, Ham?"

"You know I'm gay, right?"

"I know," she said.

After that, Ms. Vasquez and I entered into a totally new kind of relationship. It wasn't like she was a teacher anymore, or even my director. It was like she was my older sister. And I kept her secret just the way I knew that she kept mine. In rehearsals we would talk to one another as if we were partners; professionals working on a professional production, not amateurs just working on just a little school play.

I felt as though I had matured by ten years in the space of two weeks. And because of all of this, I was gaining in confidence. I felt stronger about making choices with my performance and I doubted myself less and less. I'll always remember that for as long as I live—that a teacher trusted me with such a personal thing.

As we got closer and closer to the opening of the show, I realized that I could walk into the school every day with a feeling of fearlessness. I didn't dread the school day or what the assholes in the school might say or do to me. I didn't really think anybody was treating me any differently. I could still count on being called a faggot or a homo or a queer on a regular basis. But somehow it was different now.

One Thursday I was in a study hall, sitting in the back of the room with Ezra Gold and Jacob.

Ezra was an amazing artist, and he spent a lot of time drawing comic-book characters that he created himself. The three of us had begun making a habit of coming into Brother Eugene's study hall because he never made anyone study. Most of the time he wasn't even in the room, like right now.

Ezra had done a cartoon of Darth Vader interrogating Princess Leia. In his drawing he had replaced Princess Leia's earmuff hair rolls with two reel-to-reel tape spools. The caption had Princess Leia saying: "Transmission tapes? What transmission tapes?"

"TRANSMISSION TAPES?
WHAT TRANSMISSION TAPES?"

As the three of us sat at the back of the room, our heads bent over Ezra's latest masterpiece and laughing our asses off, a senior by the name of Thomas Davenport (and a close friend of Dieter Schwarz, of course) made a grand entrance into the classroom, his major's uniform pressed and brass and boots gleaming with a high polish. He took one look at us and said, in a voice that had been trained to carry over the troops, "Jesus Christ, Sissykins. Why do you have to be such a fag?"

Clearly all thirty-some students in the room heard him. Most of the boys looked back at where we were sitting, and there were pockets of laughter in different parts of the room. Thomas smirked at me and strolled over to a desk near the front of the class. I remember thinking for just a flash that it sucked that he had such a great butt. And then I went back to looking at Ezra's drawings. Just months ago something like that would have probably destroyed me. But now it seemed to hardly matter at all.

I was starting to feel like I might be able to make it through all four years at St. Ignatius Loyola without either getting killed or jumping off of a bridge.

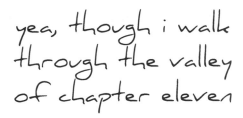

yea, though i walk through the valley of chapter eleven

It was the first full week of May—Monday, May fifth to be exact. I remember the day like I remember my name. The play was due to open on the ninth . . . just four days away.

My mom and I had gotten home a little later than usual, since rehearsals were running so long. We sat and had dinner alone together, because Dad was working late.

At about nine o'clock I was sitting at my desk in my room doing my Religion homework and listening to Fleetwood Mac's *Rumours* album when I heard my dad come home. A few minutes later there was a knock at my door.

"Come in," I said.

My dad came in the room, carrying a package under one arm.

Now normally, my dad didn't come in my room. I think I could count on both hands the total number of times he had come into my room once I was past the age of ten. But in he came, with this strange package under his arm. He stood awkwardly near the door like he was coming into the dentist's office.

"Hi, Dad. What's up?"

"Did I catch you at a bad time? 'Cause I could come back later if you're too busy."

"No, of course not. Is everything okay?"

"Sure, son. Everything's fine." He just stood there, looking at me.

"Would you like to sit down?" I gestured to the bed and turned the stereo off. He placed the package on the bed and perched stiffly at the foot of the bed, his hands dangling between his knees.

"How's the play coming?" he asked.

"Great." I said. "I'm a little nervous, but I feel like I'm pretty ready."

"Got your lines all memorized?" he said.

"Oh, yeah. Weeks ago." We looked at each other for a long moment.

I felt as though I was looking at him for the first time. He didn't seem like my father anymore. He just seemed like a guy. I was so used to seeing him as a kind of concrete foundation that our little family unit was built on. And I still saw that. But for the first time I saw an openness to him, a kind of gentleness that I had never seen before. And I realized that he was just a man trying to talk to his weird son; his son, who was this odd living thing that he had created but that was absolutely nothing like him. And I wondered if he didn't wish sometimes that he had a regular type of son: one who played ball and had to be told to clean up his room and who maybe didn't shower every single day. I wondered if maybe sometimes he wished he had someone else for a son.

"So listen," he said finally. "I know that you and I don't always understand each other." It was like he was reading my mind. "And I know I'm not very good at expressing myself. But I wanted to tell you that your mother and I are really proud of you. We both think you're a pretty special boy." His eyes started to get a little moist. He paused for a moment. Then he said, "Anyway, before I get all mushy . . . I got you something." He handed me the package.

"Should I open it now?" I said, trying hard not to get all choked up.

"Of course, Bozo!"

I opened the package.

"It's just something your mother told me you wanted. I hope you like them."

It was a new pair of combat boots, still in the army/navy surplus box.

"Dad, I don't know what to say."

"Is that something you really wanted?"

"Oh, yeah!" I said, my face breaking out in a huge grin. "These are just like the ones that the drill team members wear!"

"Try 'em on, Bozo!" I put the boots on with my T-shirt and pajama shorts and marched up and down my room, my dad and I laughing like a couple of idiots.

On Thursday, May 8 I wore my new boots for the first time. The show was opening the next night at 7 PM, and we had our last dress rehearsal in the auditorium that day immediately after the school day. But I also had corps day, so I had to wear my uniform to school. I put on my freshly cleaned and ironed uniform. I had polished the brass insignias on the uniform the night before. Then I laced up my brand new boots and carefully bloused the olive-green wool trouser legs at the tops of the boots. I looked at myself in the mirror for an embarrassingly long time.

When it was clear I would be late if I didn't get my ass in gear, I grabbed my satchel and rushed out of my room.

I stood in the living room at attention, waiting for my dad to inspect the whole ensemble. He came into the living room and saw me there, standing at attention, and he beamed with pride.

"Looking mighty sharp, corporal," he said. (I had started out as a private first class and then in February, because of my good grades and my spotless inspection record I had been promoted to corporal.)

"Thanks, Dad." I gave him a smart salute.

My mom came in just then, gave me a whistle and said, "Hubba hubba, burn some rubba! Howdy, soldier. You new in town?" She winked at me and punched me lightly on the arm. Dad and I both groaned in response.

When I got to school I was greeted by a burst of catcalls and whistles when I approached our regular table in the cafeteria.

"Yes, sir Captain Charisma, sir!" said Fritz, shooting me a crappy salute.

"Sna-zee," said Jacob. "Where'd you get the storm troopers?"

"Gee, soldier. Buy a girl a drink?" said Nels in a high falsetto voice.

"All right, all right. Settle down you smartasses." I said, grinning. "My dad gave them to me."

"They thertainly are thpiffy," said Stuart.

I walked down the halls with an added air of military pride and bearing. Suddenly I could see why Dieter and Thomas Davenport and all their pissy friends walked around the school like they owned the place. I couldn't seem to stop myself from marching from one class to another.

Everything seemed to be going really great until I headed out to the quad to join up with my company. I was marching down the stairs when I saw that the exit to the quad was blocked by a senior whose name I didn't know. I knew he was a member of the Ignatius Company Varsity Drill Team by the red cord that encircled the top of his left arm and shoulder. I stopped short at the bottom of the stairs.

"Going somewhere, homo?" said a voice behind me.

I turned and saw Porter Harrington emerge from the dark corner behind the stairs. Porter was a senior and a lieutenant. He was the executive officer of B Company, which was the company I belonged to—the same company that was currently forming ranks out on the quad for inspection and marching drills. He was also the commander of the Ignatius Company Varsity Drill Team. Behind him were two other boys. The bright red cords on their shoulders told me they were on the drill team, too.

The two other boys rushed forward and grabbed me by the arms, pulling me back into the dark area behind the stairwell. One of them clamped his hand over my mouth. Porter walked slowly up to me, cracking his knuckles. I could see the other boy who had been blocking the door standing watch at the foot of the staircase.

"You're going to keep quiet, aren't you?" Porter said. I looked at him and nodded. He signaled the boy to take his hand away from my mouth. "We're just going to have a little talk, right Corporal?"

"Yes, sir." I said quietly. The two boys released my arms but stood close behind and on either side of me.

Porter took a step closer to me and looked me up and down, like he would during an inspection. His eyes landed on my boots. "Where are your low-quarters, soldier?" he demanded, his eyes travelling back up to meet mine.

"At home, sir."

"Where did you get those boots?"

"My father gave them to me."

"My father gave them to me, what?"

"My father gave them to me, sir."

"And what makes you think you have the right to wear those boots?"

I stopped for a moment, unsure about what to say.

"These are military issue." I said slowly. "There's no rule against me having them."

He looked at the two boys on either side of me, his mouth turning up on one side into a half-sneer. Then he slowly turned his gaze back to me.

"Boots like that are for men," he said, "not piss ant little faggots like you."

The two boys on either side of me snickered. Very deliberately, Porter lifted one of his feet off the ground and dragged the boot sole across the tops of both my boots, scuffing the high gloss shine that I had worked so hard on last night. We both looked down at the scuffmarks, then Porter shook his head sadly. "It doesn't look like you're taking very good care of your boots, soldier." He took a step back from me and gave me a last inspecting glance up and down my uniform.

"I don't want to see you wearing those boots again, do you understand me?" He turned and began to walk away.

"You can't force me not to wear these. I have just as much right to wear these boots as you do," I said. I immediately knew I should have kept my mouth shut.

He turned slowly to face me again, his brow dark with fury. "What did you say to me, you little faggot?"

When I spoke, my voice was quiet and trembling. "There's no rule against me wearing these boots . . . sir."

Porter signaled his goons, who grabbed me by my arms pulling them behind my back. One of them clamped his hand on my mouth again.

"I tell you what," Porter said between clenched teeth. "Wear the fucking boots if you want to. Just be ready for a little of this every time I see you wear them." He punched me twice, hard, in the stomach, knocking the wind out of me. The boys let go of my arms and I fell to the ground, gasping for breath. Porter pulled one foot back and let loose a kick that landed squarely on my upper arm. I recoiled in pain but had no air to cry out.

"Hold him down," Porter said to his two goons. Each one planted a boot on each of my shoulders pinning me to the ground. Unable to make more than a slight gasping sound, I watched as he opened his trousers, took himself out and urinated on my boots.

"Let's see if you want to wear them now," he said, as he did up his pants. The three of them left me writhing on the floor under the stairs.

I was able to get up a few minutes later. Humiliated and sore, I slunk into the nearest bathroom and splashed water on my face. Then I took off my boots and washed them in the sink. I put them back on and threw my socks away. I stayed in the bathroom the rest of the period, sitting on the side of the basin staring at my reflection in the mirror.

But I didn't cry.

Once the period was over I managed to make it to my next class. My stomach and my shoulder hurt, but it was the *impotent*[20] anger I felt that hurt more than any physical injury.

I couldn't do anything about it.

If I told someone, then everyone would find out that Porter Harrington had pissed on my boots. I could take a couple of punches and a kick, but I didn't think I could stand the whole

---

[20]**im•po•tent** [**im**-p*uh*-t*uh*nt] *adj.* 1. without power; not potent; helpless 2. unable to engage in sexual intercourse because of the inability to achieve or keep an erection 3. *Obsolete.* unable to exercise self-restraint

When you're different or an outcast or otherwise crapped upon by society, you get used to feeling this way. At least I'm not definition #2.

school knowing I had let him pee on me (well, on my boots, not actually on me). And I couldn't bear the thought of my parents being dragged into the office and told that another boy had urinated on my boots, the boots my dad had taken so much time and trouble and money to get me.

And what if my telling someone interfered with the show?

So I kept my mouth shut. But I knew one thing for certain. I wasn't going to stop wearing those boots just because Harrington had threatened me. I would rather take a beating twice a week for the rest of my life than let him scare me into going back to my low-quarter shoes.

But for the time being I had to shove all of this shit away and focus on the show. Nothing was going to stop me from being ready for this play and from enjoying every minute of the experience.

I don't think I slept for one full hour the night before. My lines and my blocking kept running through my head over and over again. And the more I thought about the show, the more I thought about how fantastic it would feel to stand up on that stage and show everyone that I would not be beaten. And anyone who had done anything crappy to me since I had come to Loyola could suck it when I stood up on that stage and made my final bow after each performance. I would show all of them that I was more than just the names they had called me and more than what they thought of the way I walked or the way I talked or whether I liked boys or girls. Fuck'em.

The day of the first performance dragged on like some endless walk through a tar pit. Each period was longer than the one before, and by the end of the day I would've sworn the clock was actually running backwards.

The cast met in the auditorium for a last run-through of the lines, then we went up to Ms. Vasquez's room and had a pizza party, pizza courtesy of Ms. Vasquez. After we ate, we got into our costumes and makeup, each one of us ready way too early of course. We sat around Ms. Vasquez's room dressed in Elizabethan clothes and playing cards or studying lines or getting up every two minutes to check the time or check our costumes in the mirror.

Fifteen minutes before curtain, the cast stood in a circle in the hallway behind the stage, sweaty hands clasped. I knew my parents and Sammy were all out there in the audience, waiting to see me on stage.

"I want you all to have a great show tonight," said Ms. Vasquez. "Just go out there, and trust the work that we have all done to prepare for this performance. Just go out there and give it everything you've got. If something goes wrong, move past it and go on. I want you to know that I'm extremely proud of each and every one of you, and I know that you're going to be great."

We all raised our hands up and put our arms around each other and gave each other a huge group hug.

The lights changed for my first scene (scene two of the play) and I stepped out onto the stage with Claudius, Gertrude, Polonius, Laertes and a couple of attendants. I could hear my parents shout and clap and whistle when the lights hit my face.

"Take thy fair hour, Laertes," said Kenneth (Claudius), "time be thine, And thy best graces spend it at thy will! But now, my cousin Hamlet, and my son—"

"A little more than kin," I said to the audience, "and less than kind."

And with that, my first lines were spoken. And I found that my nervousness left me completely. I was no longer Charles Siskin, social outcast and school homo. I was Hamlet, Prince of Denmark.

I stood in the wings during Act II, scene 2 watching Nels and Stuart in their first scene.

"Both your majethtieth Might, by the thovereign power you have of uth, Put your dread pleasureth more into command than to entreaty," said Stuart. There was a slight sound of snickering at his lisp and I saw him shoot the crowd a dirty look.

"But we both obey, And here give up ourselves, in the full bent to lay our service freely at your feet, To be commanded," said Nels. He looked over at me standing in the wings and I gave him a thumbs up.

And the play moved on, and came successfully to its end without any major problems. I stood on the stage during the curtain call, listening to the applause and smiling from my head to my feet.

I was happy with my performance for the most part, but I

didn't think it was brilliant. I felt that it was the most I could do just to get through the thing from beginning to end. And I knew that there were three other opportunities for me to really give at least one performance that I could be completely proud of. I had three more chances to regain that feeling I had on the first day that I auditioned . . . that feeling that the words and the character and my own thoughts and feelings would all come together into one perfect combination of elements that would make the story of Hamlet real and deep and true.

After the show, the cast stood around in the hallway behind the stage, congratulating one another and laughing and reliving specific moments from the performance, little line flubs, unexpected audience responses, etc. etc. I was heading to the classroom that we had set up as a dressing room for the boys when Stuart caught up to me.

"Hey, Charleth!" he said. "Congratulationth! How do you feel?"

"I feel great," I said. "How about you?"

"I feel fantathtic!" He smiled broadly at me. "Hey, lithen. I'm inviting everyone over to my houthe after the show tomorrow for a kind of catht party. Do you think you can come?"

"Well, I have to ask my parents, but I don't see why not," I said. "I can let you know for sure tomorrow."

"Cool! Make sure you can come, okay? It wouldn't be the thame without you."

I changed out of my costume and went to meet my parents and Sammy in the lobby of the auditorium.

As I walked down the darkened school hallway, I saw a figure approaching me.

"Hey, that was some show."

It was a senior I recognized from the hallways between classes. I saw him at least a couple of times a week, but I didn't know his name. I knew he was a captain in D Company, but he had never spoken to me before.

He was a little bit taller than I was and he had red hair and blue eyes. He wasn't particularly handsome, really kind of ordinary looking. He wasn't one of the boys that I embarrassed myself by staring at on a regular basis. But I remembered his face. And I remembered that he had a great smile.

"We haven't actually met," he said. "My name is Phillip Brockett." He held his hand out to me. "I thought your performance was amazing," he said. I shook his hand, not knowing what else to do.

"Thanks," I said.

"I really enjoyed the play, but I thought you stood out head and shoulders above the rest of the cast. And not just because you were playing Hamlet. There's something about you when you're on stage. It's impossible to look away from you."

I blushed furiously and looked at my shoes. "Thank you. That really means a lot to me," I said, lamely.

"Listen. I know you don't know me from Adam. But would you let me take you out for a bite to eat after the show tomorrow? I'm planning on coming to see the show again."

I was completely *nonplussed*[21] for a moment.

"I'm sorry," he said after I was silent for a long moment.

---

[21]**non•plus** [non-**pluhs, non**-plus] *adj.(+ed)* 1. The state of confusion or disorientation *v.* (+ object) 2. To perplex or cause one to be at a loss of what to say, do or think

This word always sounds to me like the exact opposite of what it really means.

"I guess I'm being a little pushy. I'm sorry if I embarrassed you. I really liked the play and I guess I'll see you at school." He turned to walk away.

"No, wait!" I almost shouted. He turned back to face me again. "You just caught me off guard, is all," I said.

"So does that mean yes?" He smiled at me and all at once he seemed something more than just an ordinary looking guy. He seemed charming and sweet.

"Well, I'm supposed to go to a party after the show tomorrow," I said. His face fell immediately.

"Oh. Of course. I understand." We stood facing each other for a few moments, neither one of us seeming to know what to say.

"Well," he said finally, "I'll be at the show tomorrow night. Just let me know if you change your mind. I'll be hanging out in the lobby, waiting to get your autograph." He smiled that winning smile and then without a word he turned and disappeared down the hall.

"Here comes the Prince of Denmark!" my mother yelled across the lobby. Several heads turned and some people actually applauded.

Sammy came running up to me and threw her arms around me. She had a huge bouquet of flowers in one hand. "Way to go, Egghead!" she said, kissing my face over and over again. My parents caught up to her.

"I'm so proud of you," my mother said.

"That was unbelievable," said my father. "How did you memorize all those lines?" And they all three started talking at once, complimenting the show and praising my performance.

After the show we went out for dessert and coffee at a

swanky place that Sammy picked out. I had a crème brulée and an English breakfast tea.

"Hey, Mom?" I said as we finished our desserts.

"Yes, sweetheart?"

"Stuart is having a party tomorrow night after the show. Would it be all right if I went?"

"Of course it would! I think that's terrific! Will you need a ride?"

"I can probably ride over there with him and his mom. I might need to be picked up, though."

"That's no problem," she said. "Of course we'll be at the show again tomorrow night, and I don't mind coming to pick you up, even if it's late."

"Thanks, Mom."

All night long I kept thinking about meeting Phillip Brockett. I couldn't even think about the play and how happy I was about the first performance going so well. I just kept wondering, what did it all mean? Did this guy actually ask me out on a date? Or was he just being friendly? Maybe he just really liked Shakespeare and he wanted to talk about the play and about my character and stuff like that.

I was in my bed wide-awake, wondering and wondering what it all meant.

At around 1 AM I was struck by a horrible thought: What if this was some kind of cruel joke? I didn't know this Phillip Brockett, as he said, from Adam. I didn't know who he hung around with or anything. He could be best friends with Dieter Schwarz or Porter Harrington or any number of guys at school who hated my guts because they thought I was a big fag. What if this was some kind of plan to make a fool out of me? Or worse, lure me away from the school and beat the crap out of me?

I lay awake for hours going back and forth about what this whole thing with Phillip Brockett was really all about. And even if his intentions were totally honest and he was really asking me out on a date, was I going to blow off my best friend's party for the first guy who expressed any interest in me . . . some guy I didn't even know?

I finally fell asleep around three and slept until eleven the next day.

By the time my parents and I got to the school for the show that night, I still had no idea what I was going to say to Phillip Brockett when I saw him. But I knew I had to put all of that out of my head and concentrate on the night's performance.

Ms. Vasquez started us all off with a speech about the dangers of second night performances, and how it was really easy to give a sloppy, laid-back performance because you didn't have the nervous energy of opening night coursing through your veins. She led the whole cast in an energy game called "chaos tag" and after running around like lunatics for ten minutes we were all ramped up. At five minutes before seven we took our places.

I could definitely see what she was talking about. The running time of the show was feeling definitely longer than it had been the night before.

But during the show I started to feel like I was concentrating less on where I was standing or what my hands were doing or which line was coming next, and more on the actual events of the story.

During my scene with Gertrude I really began to feel enraged with her—that she could do something so low and repulsive as to marry my father's brother before my father was barely cold in his grave. And I actually felt as though I could murder Claudius to avenge my father's death.

But in spite of this progress, I still didn't feel that sense of magic that I was hoping to achieve. I wasn't quite losing myself completely in the story or the part. But maybe I was being too hard on myself. I mean, I wasn't John Barrymore or Sir John Gielgud. I was just a freshman kid in high school doing a high school play.

Once the show was over, I sat in the dressing room putting on my shoes when Stuart came up to me.

"Are you coming to the party?" he said.

I suddenly remembered the whole Phillip Brockett thing. What was I going to do about that? I had no idea.

"Let me double check with my parents," I said, hoping to buy myself some time.

"Oh." Stuart said, caught off guard for a moment. "Well let me know what you want to do. You can catch a ride with me and my mom if you want. Jutht meet uth in the lobby when you're ready."

I finished tying my shoes and made a beeline for the lobby. I needed to see if Phillip Brockett was even there. And if he was, to talk to him so I could try to figure out exactly what he was all about.

I got to the lobby from the south hallway and stood looking over the crowd. I could see Stuart's mom standing with a group of her friends at the side of the lobby farthest from me. Then I saw my parents standing near the doors to the outside, talking to each other. No sign of Phillip Brockett.

"Hey there," said a voice right next to me. It was Phillip. He was standing right next to the entrance to the south hallway, leaning casually against the wall.

"Oh, shit!" I said. "Hi!"

"I'm sorry, did I startle you?"

"Yeah, a little." I glanced over to my parents and then to Stuart's mom. None of them had seen me yet.

"Another great performance . . . even better than last night's," he said.

"Umm, thanks," I replied, a little nervously. "I really can't believe you came a second time."

"Are you kidding? Who knows? I may end up coming to every show."

I felt my face redden like a little schoolgirl's.

"So, have you made a decision about what you're going to do tonight?" he asked, still cool as a cucumber and leaning against the wall like James Dean.

"About that," I said, taking another quick look across the lobby. My mom was stepping outside, probably to smoke a cigarette, and my dad was busy looking at a big calendar of events that was posted on the wall. "Can we talk over here?" I said, motioning into the hallway where we wouldn't be seen.

"Sure," he said.

Once we were out of view of the lobby I took a deep breath and began. "See, my best friend, you know, the guy who played Rosencrantz?"

"The one with the lisp."

"Yeah. He's having a party tonight and I really think I should go."

"Sure," he said. He seemed a little let down. "Of course you want to be with your friends from the show. I think I'm being a little *obtrusive*[22]."

Oh, shit! He has a great vocabulary! And he doesn't mind using it! Suddenly he became twice as appealing.

"No! not at all," I said quickly. "It's just... you know, to be quite honest, I'm not really sure why you're even talking to me."

He grinned shyly. "I told you. I think you're an amazing actor. And I'd like the chance to get to know you a little better."

"I'm not trying to be snotty to you," I said. "I'm just not used to this kind of thing."

"What kind of thing?" He raised his eyebrows and smiled a knowing smile.

"Well, I don't even know. I mean, I'm not even really sure what kind of a thing this is."

He gave a short, soft laugh. "Are you trying to tell me you've never been asked out on a date before?" I opened my mouth, then shut it again, completely not knowing what to say. "Is that what you mean?" he prompted, smiling that sly smile again.

"Yeah. I guess so."

"So you've never been out on a date?" His smile broadened and he took a small step toward me.

"No. No, I haven't." I felt my mouth dry out and I swallowed hard.

He took another step toward me. Now we were standing practically toe-to-toe, his face just inches from mine.

"So I guess that means you've never been kissed before," he said in a soft voice.

---

[22]**ob•tru•sive** [*uh*b-**troo**-siv] *adj.* 1. acting in a forward manner or conducting oneself in such a way as to force oneself onto another through thoughts or actions 2. blatant, noisy or obvious 3. sticking out or protruding

Watch out for guys with great vocabularies.

"N—" before I could even say no, he took my chin in one hand and kissed me gently and lightly on the mouth. My breath caught in my chest.

He let go of my chin and stepped back from me. "There," he said. "now you can say you have."

I leaned back against the wall and tried to catch my breath. My mind was racing with a million thoughts. I guess this couldn't really be a cruel joke, I thought. I was pretty sure one of Dieter or Porter's friends would never go that far just to try to fool me. I guess he really wanted to go out with me.

I was suddenly aware that we were standing in the school, in a darkened hallway where anyone could come along at any moment. And I knew that Stuart and his mom and my parents were just around the corner, waiting for me.

And a boy had kissed me! And it felt amazing!

I made up my mind in a flash.

"I need to say goodbye to some people," I said, a little breathlessly. "Can I meet up with you in a few minutes?"

"Sure thing, handsome," he said, laughing lightly at my flustered state. "I'm parked in the student lot at the other end of the building. I drive a red Saab. I'll meet you there in ten." He stroked my cheek lightly with one hand and walked down the hallway.

I took a moment to collect myself, then ran into the lobby.

I looked around quickly, but my parents were nowhere to be seen. I could see Stuart and his mom talking with Nels and his parents at the other end of the lobby.

I rushed out the lobby doors and ran right into my dad, who was about to come back into the building.

"There you are," he said. "Your mother and I thought you might've left for Stuart's party without saying goodbye."

My mother was standing just outside the door, finishing her cigarette.

"I would never do that, Dad."

"That show was fantastic," she said. "Even better than last night's."

"Thanks, mom." I said, quickly. "I don't mean to rush off, but I know that Stuart and his mom are inside waiting for me. If it's okay with you, I think I'll just stay at Stuart's tonight. That way you don't have to come pick me up. The party might go pretty late."

"Is that okay with Stuart's mom?" my mother asked.

"Yeah, I just spoke to her and she says it's okay. I'm glad you enjoyed the show," I said, kissing my mom and dad hurriedly. "I'll call you tomorrow morning when I'm ready for you to come pick me up." I headed hastily back toward the doors.

"Okay," my mom yelled, smiling at my dad and shaking her head. "Have a good time!"

"Good night, son. And congratulations again!" my dad yelled at me. I barely heard his last words as I rushed back into the building.

When I came back into the lobby I could see that Stuart's mom was still talking to Nels's parents. Stuart and Nels stood off to one side. I jogged up to them, forcing myself to breath a little more easily.

"There you are," said Stuart. "Tho are you ready to go, or what?

"Listen, I said, "would you mind if I showed up a little late? My mom and dad want to take me out for a little celebration dessert."

"Didn't you guys go out last night?" Nels said. I wanted to kick him.

"That was with my mom's friend, Sammy." I said, thinking as quickly as I could. "I think they want to have a little 'family only' celebration. I promise I won't be too late."

"I gueth tho," said Stuart, a little doubtfully. "But I don't really know how long thith thing ith going to go on."

"I'll hurry things up as much as I can," I said. I was shifting my weight back and forth from one leg to the other.

"Do you have to pee or something?" Nels said. Again, just one sharp kick, right to the shin.

"No." I think I glared at Nels a little. "I just want to get going so I can get to the party."

"Okay," said Stuart. "Jutht give me a call if you're going to be really late."

"I will," I said. "Oh, Stuart! Do you think it would be all right if I spent the night at your house? That way my mom doesn't have to drive over late to pick me up."

"Hey, mom!" Stuart yelled. " Can Charleth thleep over?"

"Sure, honey," she said, without even looking away from her conversation with Nels's parents.

"Great," I said. "I've got to run. My parents are waiting for me in the car. I'll see you guys in an hour or so." I ran out the lobby doors without even waiting for a reply.

Outside the doors I took a quick left toward the student parking lot. I hoped to God that Stuart's mom would spend a few more minutes talking to Nels's parents, and that they would miss both my parents leaving the main parking lot and me skulking over to the student lot.

I hauled ass to the student lot, looking constantly over my shoulder at the lobby doors. No Stuart and his mom yet.

I could see that there was only one car in the student lot: a red Saab. I ran up to the passenger's side and got in.

"Perfect timing," Phillip said. He popped a tape into the stereo and Blondie's "Heart of Glass" started playing. He turned the volume up, started the car, and we drove away.

MAKE-OUT MOBILE

We drove in silence for a moment, listening to the music.

"Where are we going?" I said after a minute.

"What?"

"I said, where are we going?" I shouted over the music. Phillip turned the volume down slightly.

"I thought we'd hit the T.G.I. Friday's, maybe get a bite to eat or some dessert."

"That sounds great," I said.

"I know it's not very posh, but they're open late and they have a lot to choose from. Is that okay?"

"Sure." I looked out the window for a minute. Then I turned back to him suddenly. "Would you mind taking me to my friend's party later?" I said.

"Sure, no problem." I looked over at his profile as he drove. He actually was kind of handsome. His red hair was in a regulation short JROTC style and he had freckles across the bridge of his nose. His eyes were greenish blue in the light from the streetlamps. I looked around at his car. It was a couple of years old, and the leather seats were clean and worn in a comfortable and careful way.

"I like your car," I said, trying to make conversation.

"Thanks. It was my dad's. He gave it to me when he got a new one."

I couldn't think of another thing to say.

We drove on without speaking for several minutes. Blondie was followed by the B-52's then the Eurythmics.

"I really like this tape," I said. "Did you make it?"

"I did. You like new wave?"

"Sure." I really did.

Thank God I could see the T.G.I. Friday's coming up on the left. I felt sure that if I kept up this *inane*[23] conversation he was going to shove me out of the moving car and leave me by the side of the road.

The restaurant was next to a large shopping mall. We turned into the restaurant parking lot, but instead of driving close to the restaurant, he drove around the side of the building and as far from the door as he could get. He pulled into a parking slot that was mostly in shadow, equally distant between two large arc sodium lights. There were no other cars anywhere near us. Behind us was the blank brick wall of the restaurant and in front of us was a vast desert of empty mall parking lot.

---

[23]**in•ane** [ih-**neyn**] *adj.* 1. empty, insubstantial; feeble or flimsy 2. without meaning or point; silly

Even after all the books I've read and all the writing I've done, in the presence of even a halfway cute boy I clearly become the King of Inane Conversation.

I took off my seatbelt and started to get out of the car.

"Hey, hold on a second," he said, reaching across me and pulling my door closed. "What's your hurry?"

"Oh. No hurry." I said. I settled back in my seat.

"Good," he said and kissed me again on the mouth. I felt like a stick of butter, melting in a hot pan. He ran his hand through my hair. "I thought you were terrific up on that stage," he whispered to me, and kissed me again. I was finding it difficult to breath. He looked intently into my eyes for a moment, then touched my lips with his fingers. "Were you telling me the truth when you said you've never been on a date before?" he said, stroking my neck.

"No. Never. Hard to believe, huh?"

He chuckled softly. "Very," he said, mockingly.

"As God is my witness," I said, uncomfortable with his direct gaze, but somehow unable to look away.

"And no one's really ever kissed you before?" he said, kissing me again.

"My mother used to kiss me good night," I said. (I left out every single night of my life until last year.)

"That's not the kind of kiss I meant," he said, kissing me more deeply.

"Certainly not like this," I said, once my mouth was free.

"So then, I can assume," he said, moving even closer to me and putting his hand on my thigh, "you've never done anything else?" I let out a soft little "oh" at the touch of his hand. "Is this okay?" he asked.

"Sure," I said.

"And I guess that means you've never done anything like this?" He slid his other hand into my shirt and across my chest.

"Anything like what?" I gasped, marveling at how hot his hand felt on my skin.

"I tell you what," he said, "why don't we get into the back seat, where we can be more comfortable?"

Ten minutes (or was it several hours?) later we were back sitting in our places in the front seat and he was doing up his jeans.

I wasn't able to sort out how I was feeling.

I was out of breath, like I had just run a long distance. My hands gripped the seat tightly and my knuckles were white with humiliation. And I felt cheated, dissatisfied, and *exploited*[24]. I tucked my shirt into my pants, which had never even gotten unbuttoned.

"Do you still want to get something to eat?" He sounded completely different from before.

"No," I said quietly. "Can you just take me to my friend's?"

"Sure," he said, his voice devoid of any emotion, his hand turning the key to start the car.

"Can we stop at a Seven Eleven?" I said. "I want to get some gum."

We finished the rest of the ride in almost complete silence, except for me telling him to turn here or turn there. I asked him to pull over around the corner from Stuart's house. It was just before midnight.

We sat in the car, the engine idling.

"I had a really great time," he said, all charm and appeal gone from his voice.

---

[24]**ex•ploit** [ek-**sploit**] *v.* 1. to make use of, especially for profit: *the corporation exploited the availability of cheap goods and labor.* 2. to utilize or make constructive use of: to exploit your own talents. 3. to take advantage of

The less said about this word, the better.

"Thanks," I said, not believing that I was saying it, even as I was saying it.

"Maybe we can get together again sometime," he said, finally looking at me for the first time since we had gotten to the restaurant.

"Sure," I said. Again, I couldn't believe these words were coming out of my mouth. Why was I saying that? I should have told him that I hoped I would never see him again as long as I lived. I should have said he was a snake and that I felt like I needed about twelve hot showers. But I just sat there and stared straight ahead as he took a pen out of the glove compartment and wrote his number on a piece of paper.

He handed it to me and said: "Call me any time if you want to get together again."

"Thanks," I said again. I wanted to punch myself in the face.

I got out of the car and he drove away without another word or even a backward glance.

I stood there on the sidewalk for a minute, then walked around the corner to Stuart's house.

"Charleth!" Stuart said when he opened the door. "I was thtarting to think you had bailed on uth."

"I wouldn't miss it for the world," I said.

cross my heart
and hope to die, stick
chapter twelve in my eye

My mom picked me up from Charles's house at around noon on Sunday. I had split my time at the party between sleepwalking and putting on a happy face so that I wouldn't spoil anyone else's time. At least once or twice Stuart and Nels asked me if I was okay. Jacob and Fritz were there and didn't seem to notice anything out of the ordinary.

That night, after everyone had left the party, Stuart asked me one more time if everything was okay, and I lied and told him I was fine.

But I spent most of that night awake, going over and over the events in my mind.

As Sunday dragged on, Saturday began to seem more and more like it had happened to someone else. The more I thought about it, the more I questioned how I felt about the whole thing. I mean, was it really all that bad? Maybe that's the way your first time is supposed to be. And could it really be called my first time at all? How did you define a thing like that? And when you get right down to it, what was I really so upset about? It wasn't like I was in love with the guy. I barely knew him. It wasn't like we had been dating for a month and I thought we were going to spend the rest of our lives together and then he used me like a wad of Kleenex and tossed me aside.

Maybe that was what made me so angry about the whole thing. I had let it happen. I was taken in by a few compliments and a charming smile and I let it happen. Surely I could have stopped things anytime I wanted. But I didn't. So I really had no one to blame but myself.

By the time Monday rolled around, I had convinced myself that I was just being a big baby about the whole thing. After all, he had given me his phone number. And he told me to call him if I wanted to get together again. Maybe it was just "one of those things" (whatever that meant). And besides, he was the one who had come up to me. He had come to see the show twice . . . and had told me what a great performance I had given. Clearly I was making too much out of nothing.

By Wednesday I hadn't seen Phillip at all, and my imagination had completely taken over. I had pushed all the shame and humiliation I had felt that night back to the furthest part of my mind. I kept trying to convince myself that something wonderful had happened, and that I didn't really understand the way these kinds of things worked. He hadn't meant to make me feel bad. He had even offered to go into the restaurant and get something to eat. And he had given me his number. I was even starting to think that maybe Phillip and I might start dating.

I know. I know. I get it now. But what the hell did I know then? I was just a kid.

The funny thing about all of it was that before, during, and after, I was never really actually attracted to Phillip Brockett in a romantic way. Looking back on it now, I was much more taken with Phillip Brockett as an idea. I think I wanted so desperately to have the experience of infatuation that I made myself believe that I was infatuated with him, when I was really only infatuated with the idea of him, the idea of having someone to daydream about, someone to call on the phone, someone whose name I could write all over my notebook and whose picture I could hang in my locker. I had seen other boys have that and I wanted it, too. It didn't matter if it was Phillip Brockett or the Hunchback of Notre Dame.

So before I knew what was happening, I found myself doing something really stupid.

On Thursday I started looking all over the school for him and asking seniors if they had seen him. I knew he was in the building because I had seen his red Saab in the student parking lot. But before school and after homeroom I hadn't see him anywhere. I felt myself like a snowball rolling down a steep hill, growing bigger and bigger and gaining speed as I plunged towards the bottom. And all the while I was watching myself as though I was standing somewhere off to the side, totally detached and free of any emotions or personal feelings.

Objectively.

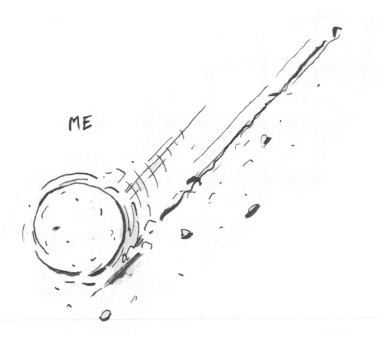

That's not really the right word. Removed. Removed from the whole situation. The whole time I knew that I was acting like an idiot, and yet somehow I was not willing or not caring to stop myself.

As I stood in Brother Marvin's room waiting for class to begin, I saw Dieter Schwarz come in and I walked right up to him.

"Hey, Dieter," I said.

"What do you want, Sissykins?" He seemed pretty surprised that I was talking to him.

"Do you know a guy named Phillip Brockett?"

"Yeah. Why?"

"Have you seen him today?"

"I don't know," he said scornfully. "What do you care?"

"I want to talk to him. If you see him will you tell him I'm looking for him?"

"Are you fucking kidding me?" He pushed me out of his way and went to his desk.

And I should have taken my warning right there.

But I didn't.

And off to the side was that other me, leaning against the wall with his arms crossed, watching me and shaking his head.

And two periods later I saw Thomas Davenport in the hall and did the same exact thing. And from a distance that other me watched, buried his face in one hand, then turned and walked away.

By fifth period I had asked at least three other seniors if they had seen Phillip and if they saw him to tell him I was looking for him.

By the end of the next day he found me at my locker and pulled me into an empty classroom.

"What the fuck is your problem?" he hissed.

"What do you mean?" I asked, knowing exactly what he meant and yanking my arm out of his vicelike grip.

"I've had a hundred people tell me you've been looking for me. What the hell do you think you're doing?"

"I just wanted to talk to you," I said, hating myself and hating the whining way my voice sounded.

"That's what the phone number was for, you moron! If you wanted to meet up again, you could've just called me. Now everyone in the school knows the little faggot Sissykins is looking for me. So I'm only going to tell you this once. Lose my number. Don't even think about calling me. And if you even so much as try to talk to me in this school or say my name to anyone I'll find you and slit your throat. Do you understand me?"

He hadn't laid a hand on me, but it felt like he had slapped me across the face. He left me standing alone in the classroom. I noticed that before he left the room he looked up and down the hall to see if anyone had seen him take me into the room or if anyone was watching him leave.

I waited for a few minutes, then left the classroom and slowly went to my locker and got my books.

I walked down the hall and down the stairs to the main entrance of the building. Across the foyer I could see Phillip standing with a group of senior boys, including Thomas Davenport. I turned quickly and stood facing the wall. I could hear a loud burst of laughter coming from the group of boys. When I turned around again, Phillip had gone.

"Hey, Sissykins!" Thomas called out to me. "Why didn't you ask me? I would've let you." He licked his lips and grabbed his crotch and the boys erupted in laughter again. I turned and walked toward the other exit farther down the hall.

I had never been so afraid in my whole life. What had I done? And more importantly, why had I done it? How could I have been such an idiot? And what was going to happen to me now? Clearly Phillip told those senior boys something. But what could he have said that wouldn't make him look just as guilty as me?

And then it came to me.

He told them all that I had asked him if I could do *that* to him. That had to be it. And of course everyone was going to believe him. Because I was Charles Sissykins, the school homo. Why wouldn't I just walk up to him and ask him if I could? After all, I had spent the whole year leering at every boy in school, and they all knew it.

I felt as though I had stepped into the path of an oncoming train, like I had just laid down on the tracks and was waiting patiently for it to squash me messily into pulp. With one insane sweep I had wiped out any ground I had made for myself by doing the play. And for the rest of my time at Loyola I would be branded even more deeply than I had been before.

I sat in the dressing room that night, filled with dread about what might happen during the performance. I felt like everyone would know and maybe when I stepped out onto the stage that night they would boo and hiss or throw rotten fruit or something.

What would my parents (who were coming to see a third performance) think when I stepped out onto the stage and was pelted with tomatoes or maybe even stones, like that woman who committed adultery that Jesus saves in the Gospel According to John? I would stand there and they (and everyone else) would know who and what I was. And they would finally know what I had been made to endure for the last eight or nine years of my life.

Just before the curtain, Ms. Vasquez came in and saw me sitting at my dressing station, staring into one of the mirrors that had been set up for the actors.

"Is everything okay, Charles?" she said gently. I wanted to blurt the whole thing out and tell her every gory detail and ask her what I should do. But the room was filled with students and I knew there was no time.

"Yeah," I said. "Everything's fine. I'm just getting into character."

"Oh. Well I'll leave you alone."

Twenty minutes later I stood in the wings, watching as the lights dimmed in the auditorium and came up on the stage. So far everything seemed to be normal.

As I stood there in the wings, my stomach wrenched in knots, I began to walk away from myself. And I felt myself drifting further and further away and floating upward toward the ceiling. And as I looked down I could see this pale, skinny boy, standing at the side of the stage, waiting to make his entrance. I watched him step onto the stage and I saw that he wasn't a boy. He was a prince. A prince burdened with more emotions than he knew how to handle: the death of his father, the marriage of his mother to his father's brother.

As the play progressed, I felt myself float down and join up with that troubled young man on the stage so that the two of us became one. One fragile human shell that was trying to contain within itself a boiling pot of emotions and events and triumphs and mistakes. A container that was too frail to hold the excess of feelings that it was being asked to hold.

It is act three. It is late day in a room of the castle at Elsinore. Gertrude, Polonius, and Claudius, hearing my approach, have just left and Ophelia stands nearby, pretending to read a book.

I come in, but don't see her. I am alone and speak aloud to myself.

And for the first time it all comes into focus. The words, whose meanings I have known with my head, I now know with my heart and with my soul. It seems perfectly natural to me that I would speak my thoughts aloud:

To be, or not to be: that is the question:
Whether 'tis nobler in the mind to suffer
The slings and arrows of outrageous fortune,
Or to take arms against a sea of troubles,
And by opposing end them? To die: to sleep;
No more; and by a sleep to say we end
The heart-ache and the thousand natural shocks
That flesh is heir to, 'tis a consummation
Devoutly to be wish'd. To die, to sleep;
To sleep: perchance to dream: ay, there's the rub;
For in that sleep of death what dreams may come
When we have shuffled off this mortal coil,
Must give us pause: there's the respect
That makes calamity of so long life;
For who would bear the whips and scorns of time,
The oppressor's wrong, the proud man's contumely,
The pangs of despised love, the law's delay,
The insolence of office and the spurns
That patient merit of the unworthy takes,
When he himself might his quietus make
With a bare bodkin? who would fardels bear,
To grunt and sweat under a weary life,
But that the dread of something after death,
The undiscover'd country from whose bourn
No traveller returns, puzzles the will

And makes us rather bear those ills we have
Than fly to others that we know not of ?
Thus conscience does make cowards of us all;
And thus the native hue of resolution
Is sicklied o'er with the pale cast of thought,
And enterprises of great pith and moment
With this regard their currents turn awry,
And lose the name of action.

And somewhere in there I understood what the whole acting thing was all about; how it was the perfect marrying of actor and character and how both of those people have to exist at once within the same person. And I felt that same feeling of coming together that I felt on the day that I auditioned for Ms. Vasquez. And as the play went on I saw the lights and the stage and the other members of the cast at the same time that I saw the castle and the king and the ghost of my father.

And when it was over I felt like I had lived two lives. I felt limp and weak and drained of every thought and emotion that had been tearing at me since earlier that day. And as the curtain rose for our final bow, I heard a roar of applause. And the curtain came down and Ms. Vasquez ran onto the stage and asked the cast to clear the stage. And the curtain came up again and I was alone on the stage and the audience stood up as one and thundered and yelled and whistled love to me like I had never felt before. And for one blazing moment I felt that everything was perfect and complete.

When it was over, Ms. Vasquez came up to me in the hallway behind the stage, fighting through the members of the cast and crew who were congratulating me and hugging me and clapping me on the back.

"Jesus Christ!" she said. "Where did all of that come from?"

And although I knew exactly where it had come from, the only answer possible was the shortest one: "I don't know," I said.

My theatrical victory burned hot and dazzling, but brief. The cast and crew laughed and joked with me about when I would be headed to Broadway. Then I changed and headed out to the lobby, where a surprising number of people from the audience had stayed around to congratulate me on a job well done.

Phaedre had come to see the show and brought me a bouquet of roses.

"That was frigging unbelievable," she said, and kissed me right on the mouth.

Of course my parents raved all the way home about what a different show it was tonight; how different and how much older I had seemed on stage. And how meaningful the words had sounded.

But by the time I was alone in my room with nothing but my own thoughts for company, the catastrophic events of the day began to play themselves over and over in my mind. And all that night as I lay in bed and all the next day as I kept myself busy, killing time until it was time to go to the school for the last show, I felt a growing sense of dread about what would happen to me at school on Monday.

"Now, you're sure you don't mind that your father and I aren't going to see the last show?" my mother asked, worriedly as they drove me to the school for the last show on Saturday night.

"For the five millionth time, Mom, it's fine. I mean you saw three performances. If you have to sit through one more show you'll both probably throw up."

"We never should have made dinner plans tonight, Peter," she said to my father, her brow furrowed with concern.

"Relax, Adriana. I'm sure Charles would tell us if it really bothered him. Wouldn't you, Son?"

"Listen to your husband, Adriana," I said, trying to lighten the mood.

"Besides," my father said, "the people from the New York office are leaving tomorrow and this is the only chance we'll have to do anything social before they go."

"And you're sure that Stuart's mom can give you a ride home?" my mother asked.

"Yes, Mom. I asked him after the show last night."

"I still feel awful," my mother said.

"Well, if it makes you feel any better, I can't see how I could possibly top last night."

My parents dropped me off and I took the sidewalk that led around to the side of the building where the cast and crew always entered. The sidewalk ran next to the student parking lot, and as I walked I looked to my right and saw a group of boys leaning in a row against a black Trans Am. Dieter Schwarz and Thomas Davenport were right in the middle.

"Hey, Sissykins," said Dieter. "Can't wait to see the show tonight. Break a leg." The boys all snickered in response and one of them brought his fist to his mouth, making a lewd gesture.

I turned and kept walking, pretending not to notice them. So this was it. They were planning something. But what? And what could I do about it? I couldn't tell anyone since they hadn't done anything yet. And what proof did I have? A wish of good luck and a filthy gesture? Maybe they were just trying to scare me. Maybe they just wanted me to get all distracted and screw up my lines or fall off the stage or something.

Whatever the case, it was clear that there was absolutely nothing I could do to stop them. I was just going to have to wait and see.

By fifteen minutes to curtain I was in a total panic. I broke one of Ms. Vasquez's basic rules and snuck out onto the stage so that I could peek through the side of the curtain and see into the house.

The auditorium was practically filled to capacity and not everyone had taken their seats yet. I scanned the audience quickly and spotted Thomas sitting at the far left. None of his pals was sitting near him. I looked to the far right side of the auditorium and saw Dieter several rows from the front. Two sets of girls sat on either side of him and he was smiling and talking to the girl on his right. I looked all across the audience and up into the balcony, but I wasn't sure who those other boys had been who I had seen out in the parking lot.

The audience was filled with parents and teachers and students from both schools. I looked back at Thomas and tried to see if he had anything with him, a bag or a backpack. But he had nothing. As far as I could tell Dieter had nothing with him either.

Maybe this was what they had intended all along . . . to make me think they were going to do something and get me so freaked out that I wouldn't be able to think straight. If that was the plan, it was working beautifully. I moved away from the curtain and headed toward the back hall.

Goddamnit I was not going to let them get into my head! I took several deep breaths and shook my arms and legs out. By now the rest of the cast was assembling for the warm-up. Ms. Vasquez joined the circle and addressed the group.

"I want you all to know that this has been an amazing experience for me. You all have met and exceeded my every expectation and you should be very proud of the work that you've done.

"A couple of things that I want you to remember. This is our last performance. This play will never be performed in exactly this way again. And it will probably be a performance that you will remember for a long time. I only say this because I want you to trust what we've created. This isn't the time for any last minute surprises or any new bits of business that you may have been holding back. The show is fantastic the way it is. Keep it fresh and new, but don't throw your fellow actors off by doing something crazy that you've never done before. It's unprofessional and unfair to the people who are trusting you.

"Secondly, I want you to enjoy yourselves. Last night's show was pretty amazing, and I know that you can capture that same magic tonight. Listen to each other, respond and react; let your nerves and your energy feed your performance.

"I won't ask you to make me proud. You've already done that. Just go out there and tell the story that Shakespeare wrote. Make Shakespeare proud. And yourselves, too." She began to tear up a little. "Now let's go out there and play the shit out of this thing!"

The cast erupted into a huge yell and we clapped hands and scattered to our places.

I put Dieter and Thomas and their stupid friends out of my mind and focused on recapturing that same feeling I had had the night before. And I think I was able to do it. I could feel that same feeling of being two people at the same time, and when I walked out onto the stage I could see the castle and the court around me. Deep in the back of my mind I was wondering if something awful was going to happen, but I refocused my eyes and ears on everything that was going on around me. I could feel that knot of emotions that had been the source of last night's performance, and I channeled it into my thoughts and words and actions.

Before I knew it, it was the first part of the original Act III and we were watching the play within a play. And nothing horrible had happened.

The original *Hamlet* is separated into five acts, but Ms. Vasquez had divided our version of the play in half, into two acts, and placed an intermission in the middle of the original Act III, right after Claudius flips out after seeing the murder of Gonzago in the play within the play. The other characters exited and I finished our Act I:

"Why, let the stricken deer go weep, the hart ungalled play; for some must watch, while some must sleep: so runs the world away."

The lights dimmed and the curtain came down and I let out a huge sigh of relief as I walked off the stage.

We began our second act and I had all but forgotten to worry that Herr Schwarz and his hoods were going to try something.

Everything started fine, and I was coming up to one of my favorite speeches.

Polonius and Rosencrantz and Guildenstern had just left the stage, leaving me alone.

"'Tis now the very witching time of night," I said, "when churchyards yawn and Hell breathes out contagion to this world . . . "

"Fag."

I heard the word lowed deeply and soft, but perfectly clear as it sailed above the audience. I paused and there was a rustling as the people in the audience shifted in their seats. I went on:

"Now could I drink hot blood . . . " I heard a sucking sound from somewhere off to the right of the house, followed by a 'shhh!'

I felt the color begin to drain from my face.

" . . . and do such bitter business as the day would quake to look on."

"Faggot." Louder this time and from the balcony, followed by a louder "shhh!"

"Soft! Now to my mother."

Someone coughed and spat the word "homo!" from the back of the auditorium, which was followed by a snickering sound.

"O heart . . . O heart.." I faltered for a moment. "O heart, lose not thy nature; let me be cruel, not unnatural . . . "

"Queer!" two voices said at once and a spattering of laughter sprayed up from the crowd. I stopped for a full ten seconds, unsure about what the next words were. I could see Clark Rudnick, the stage manager, off to my right, and hear him whispering something furiously into his headset.

"I will speak daggers to her, but use none; my tongue . . . "

"Will blow me!"

Louder laughter from the crowd and I could see several adults stand up and look around. One man in the front row left his seat and jogged toward the back of the house.

" . . . and be hypocrites . . . and soul be hypocrites in this . . . and soul in this be hypocrites . . . "

Then all at once, several voices barked "faggot!" There were huge bursts of laughter from every part of the auditorium and a chorus of shushes and a mixture of cries whose words were unclear.

And through all of this I stood in the center of the stage, alone. My whole body felt like it was made of lead and my face made of fire, shame burning in my cheeks and all around my neck. I opened my mouth but no sound came out and I could feel my hands move up my body as if they belonged to someone else, like they were two things made of clay that were not part of me.

Suddenly the lights went up in the auditorium and all sound ceased as every face, every set of eyes turned toward me. And for a moment that felt like an eternity I could see a sea of faces staring at me, their eyes and mouths wide open with astonishment. I saw Dieter Schwarz off to my left hunched down in his seat stifling his laughter and Thomas Davenport off to my right biting his arm to keep himself from cracking up. The rest of the audience was all watching me to see what I would do, but I was helpless. Fear and embarrassment had caused roots to sprout from my feet. And as I stood there, naked and exposed, I felt my eyes expand in my skull and I knew that I was going to cry and I wanted to shout out to someone to help me but my mouth was crammed with cotton. I knew that if I cried that the final nail would be hammered into my coffin, the coffin that I had lain in my whole life, waiting for this moment to arrive.

And then the curtain mercifully started to come slowly down and I could feel the hot tears begin to run down my cheeks. And I knew that the last image they were seeing was this pathetic, miserable clown that had been slaughtered on an altar for their amusement.

When the curtain finally came to rest on the stage floor I heard the crowd begin to babble. I felt someone's arms around me, leading me off the stage. I shambled along, as if sleepwalking, and I could hear Brother Baker on the PA system as he called for quiet. As I left the backstage area I could hear his first words as he addressed the crowd: "I want you all to know that I am severely disappointed in the conduct of certain members of the audience this evening. I would like the parents to know that Loyola is not the kind of school that permits this kind of deplorable behavior, and every effort will be made to locate the persons responsible . . . "

His voice faded away as I stepped out into the back hallway and I could see that it was Clark Rudnick who was leading me to the dressing room. I staggered to my dressing area and clutched the back of my chair, finally able to draw a breath. Then I felt my legs give way as the room spun one way and then the other. At last the light began to dim and the room faded away as I crumpled to the ground, out cold.

just chapter thirteen

Brother Sullivan drove me home that night in the school's station wagon.

He led me into the house and waited patiently while I changed out of my clothes and showered and put on my pajamas. Then he stood at the doorway of my bedroom as I climbed into my bed. He came forward and brushed my hair off of my forehead.

"Are you sure you're all right?" he said.

"I'm fine, Brother," I murmured. "I'm just really, really tired."

He sat on the edge of my bed.

"You're an amazing young man," he said, and smiled weakly at me. I turned my head to face the wall.

He waited around for my parents to get home and explained to them everything that had happened. Even though I was only passed out for a few seconds, everyone had agreed that the show had to be stopped and I needed to be taken home.

Over the next couple of days my parents made trips back and forth to the school, meeting with Brother Baker and with Principal Crowley. There had been no way to identify the students responsible. The auditorium was dark and what had seemed like a century to me had actually happened all too quickly. No other students came forward to identify the guilty parties.

The administration agreed that they would allow me to stay out of school the rest of the year since there were only two weeks left to the school year anyway. I could take my final exams over the summer. The school would refund my tuition and arrangements would be made for me to enroll in James Madison the following year, if that was what we decided we wanted to do.

My parents asked me again and again if I knew who had done this awful thing and I lied and told them that I had no idea. And though I was pretty sure they knew I wasn't telling the truth, I kept insisting that I didn't know who the boys were and they finally backed off and let the matter drop.

What little strength or courage I had built up over the years had been ripped clean away from me. Any other hurts or humiliations I had suffered in the past seemed tiny and insignificant when I compared them to the disaster of that night. To be so completely and publicly brought down was all the worse because of the high I had experienced the night before.

And what was even more terrible to me was the knowledge that I had brought it on myself. It was as if I had handed those boys a knife and then stretched out my neck and goaded them to draw the blade across my throat. I had drawn the target onto my own forehead, and for what? For some repulsive boy with the morals of a goat. A boy I didn't know, I didn't really like, and worse who I knew, deep down, didn't like me. Why had I done it? Was it because somewhere in my twisted head I felt like I deserved to be executed? That because I knew I was a freak? That maybe I knew I was getting what I had coming to me? After all, it was true what they had been saying about me all my life. I was a faggot. I liked boys. I was some kind of mutant thing that only lived because my mother hadn't had the sense to drown me at birth.

I stayed in bed for four whole days.

Early on the evening of the fourth day, just as the sun was beginning to go down, I heard a knock on my door.

"Charles?" my mother called through the door.

"Go away," I said. It had been my stock answer over the past four days.

"Honey, there's someone here to see you."

"I don't want to see anybody," I groaned.

There was a muffled exchange of words.

"I'm not anybody," I heard Phaedre say from the other side of the door. "Can I come in?"

"I don't care," I said after a long silence.

The door opened slowly and Phaedre came in.

She looked around at the messy, darkened room. "Jesus, this place looks like someone died in here." I didn't answer her. "Can I at least open the curtains?"

"I don't care," I sighed.

She walked over to the window, stepping over piles of books and clothes, and flung open the curtains. Bright sunlight streamed in the window, filling the room with a warm, yellow glow. "If it's okay with you, I think I'm going to open this window," she said, tartly. "No offense, but it smells a little like boy feet in here."

"I don't care." I said, turning my face to the wall. She opened the window and a gust of fresh air blew gently into the room.

"That's a little better," she said. "At least I won't suffocate from the fumes." She stood by the window for a moment, then took a couple of steps closer to the bed. "So everybody in Creative Writing is wondering what happened to you," she said, finally. "Brother Marvin doesn't have the same spring in his step since you've been gone."

I stayed turned to the wall, my face buried in my pillow.

"Are you ever going to come back to school?"

I didn't move.

"Can you at least turn over here and look at me? I mean, I did come all this way, after all."

I turned slowly and scowled mildly in her direction.

"Your mom tells me you've been holed up in here since Saturday night."

I just looked at her.

"We'd all really like it if you came back to school," she said quietly.

"I can't come back," I croaked.

"Why not?"

"Didn't you hear what happened?"

"Yeah, I heard."

"It would be too humiliating."

"It was pretty terrible," she said.

"It was the worst thing that's ever happened to me."

"Really?" Phaedre said, simply.

I turned my face away from her again. "Yeah. Really."

"I don't know. You've told me some pretty sick stories about things that have happened to you."

"Not like this."

"I don't know," she said. "It seems to me that you've had to deal with some really awful things, and you've always lived to tell the tale."

I sat up quickly and glared furiously at her. "Not like this!" I screamed at her. "I was degraded and humiliated . . . *in front of an audience!* Ridiculed and belittled like I was some kind of worthless piece of trash!"

She flinched at my attack and took a step back. I turned violently away from her and faced the wall again.

There were several minutes of near silence, broken only by my heavy breathing.

After a while she finally spoke again. Her voice was calm and low and soothing.

"But you're not a worthless piece of trash, are you?" she said. "And if you crawl away and leave without standing up for yourself, then they will have had the last word. And the only thing everyone will remember is how they got the better of you." She was quiet for a moment, then I heard her walk softly to the door. Then I heard her stop.

"And you know what else I noticed, Charles?" she said. "As awful as it may have been, the world didn't come to an end."

I heard her leave the room and shut the door behind her.

I lay there for another full hour without moving. My mother came by the room and knocked but I didn't answer.

Finally, I turned away from the wall and looked at the setting sun as it streamed through my window.

After a while I got up and went quietly into the bathroom, undressed and climbed into the shower. I turned the water on as hot as I could stand it and stood under it until my skin turned red.

After I had cleaned the film of the last four days off my body, I went back to my room and put on a fresh T-shirt and a pair of shorts. I combed my hair and looked at myself for a moment in my dresser mirror. I noticed that I needed a haircut.

I opened the door to my room and walked down the hall to the living room. My mom and dad were sitting on the sofa, reading the paper. They both noticed me at the same time and put their papers down slowly.

"Charles?" my mother said.

"Hi," I mumbled. "What are we having for dinner?"

―――――――――――――

My parents tried to talk me out of going back to Loyola, but I stood firm and refused to be discouraged.

I asked my mom to drop me off extra early the next day so that I could speak with Brother Baker before the day began. She and my father wanted to come with me, but I told them that it was something that I needed to do myself. My mother thought it was a pretty bad idea, but thank God my dad told me that he understood and after he talked it over with my mom they both went along with my decision.

I walked into the school and the main foyer was completely empty. There wouldn't be any students around for at least half an hour. I looked around at the front hall. It was pretty strange to me that it seemed to have changed since just a few days ago. It seemed smaller somehow and naked without any students rushing around. I looked up at the high ceilings and then stopped to look at the senior class pictures that were hung across one long wall. They went back to 1907, when the school was first founded. I stood looking at year after year of young men who had graduated from the school, and thought about how before I had thought they looked so old the first time I had seen them. The earliest pictures showed handsome young men in starched collars with their hair slicked down and parted in the middle. At that time they had all looked like bankers or lawyers to me. Now they just seemed like serious young men. And I could imagine my picture up on the wall with theirs some day, looking serious and scholarly and ready to meet the world.

I went into the main office and Brother Baker and Principal Crowley were able to meet with me right away. I told them that I would be finishing out the year and that it was my plan to return to Loyola the following year. I think it really caught them off guard, but I assured them that I wasn't going to let what had happened stop me from doing what I had come here to do in the first place: I was going to get my education and graduate and go to college and I wasn't going to let anyone cheat me out of that. When we finished our meeting, we all shook hands like adults and Brother Baker told me that I was a fine young man.

By the time the meeting was finished and I came out of the main office, the front hall was beginning to show some life. A few boys were walking in the front doors and through the foyer to the adjoining halls. A couple of them looked at me strangely, but no one said anything to me.

I headed down the stairs into the cafeteria to find the table where my friends and I usually hung out.

Stuart and Jacob and Fritz sat at our regular table playing a lazy game of spades. Stuart saw me first.

"Hey, Charleth," he said, concentrating hard on his hand and throwing down a card. The other boys looked up, then looked back at the cards in their hands.

"Hey, Charles," they said.

"We were wondering when you were going to get your lazy ass back to school," Fritz said.

"Yeah," said Stuart. "I told them you were probably faking thick tho you could mith your finalth." Jacob discarded and Stuart took the trick.

"Where's Nels?" I said.

They all seemed to pause for a moment. Then Stuart said: "He doethn't thit with uth anymore. He wath all pithed off becauthe he thought you ruined the clothing night, tho we told him he could go fuck himthelf." They all looked up at me, and then they smiled.

After first bell I walked up the three flights of stairs to homeroom. Now, instead of me staring at cute boys, everybody was staring at me. Nobody seemed to have the guts to actually say anything to me, but it was clear that they were very interested in the fact that I was even walking the halls of good ol' St. Lo.

I reached the third floor and turned left down the hall towards Brother Marvin's room. Brother Marvin was standing right outside the room in his usual spot, policing the goings on in the crowded hallway. He saw me as soon as I turned the corner. I walked up to him and stood facing him, looking up slightly, because he was a lot taller than I was.

He looked over the tops of his glasses at me. "*Mr. Siskin*," he said, nodding slightly.

"Brother Marvin," I replied, bowing *imperceptibly*[25].

---

[25]**im•per•cep•ti•ble** [im-per-**sep**-t*uh*-b*uh*l] *adj.* 1. not able to be perceived by the mind or the senses 2. insubstantial, faint or happening bit-by-bit

I got this word right on a Brother Marvin Word of the Day challenge. He gave me a Snicker's bar.

"Just because you've missed a couple of days doesn't mean you get an extension on your final writing project," he said sternly. *"I suspect you will have a great deal to write about."* He winked at me and gave me a wry half-smile.

When homeroom was over, Brother Marvin went out into the hall to make his customary policeman's rounds. Once he left I sat in my desk, silently preparing myself for what I knew was coming. I took my notebook out of my bag and put it back several times, just so I could feel like I was doing something as I waited for Dieter Schwarz to arrive. I wasn't sure what was going to happen, but I wanted to prepare myself for anything.

Howard Ionazzi and Joe Ramirez came in and greeted me with huge smiles and enthusiastic hellos, as if I had returned to class from a nasty bout of tuberculosis. Amanda Rice came in, ran up to me and gave me a huge hug and whispered in my ear: "You're my hero," she said.

Phaedre came in a moment later and stood smiling at me from the doorway. She strolled up to me and tousled my hair as she passed by my desk to sit in the desk behind me. "Thank God you decided to take a shower," she said as she sat down.

Then, just before the bell rang, Dieter came in. For a fleeting moment I had the thought that it had all almost been worth it to see the way he stopped cold in his tracks when he saw me, his mouth open with astonishment. I think it was the only time I had ever seen the real him, as opposed to the careful mask of control that he usually wore. It was a single second of pure surprise and bewilderment. And for that moment the cold handsomeness of his face was replaced with an exposed, tender quality that was younger and not so hard and almost beautiful. Then he covered it back up with his typical disguise of arrogance and scorn. He looked down his nose at me and opened his mouth as if he was going to say something, then he stopped and looked around the room. I saw that everyone was looking right at him, their faces set with a challenge that seemed to say: "Go ahead, you son of a bitch. Just try it." I felt Phaedre's hand on my shoulder. There was an instant of suffocating tension in the room, and then he closed his mouth and dropped his eyes to the floor.

"*Have you forgotten where your desk is, Mr. Schwarz?*" Brother Marvin said as he came into the room and that moment of suspense was broken.

Dieter started as if he had been prodded from behind.

"No, Brother," he said finally and sat down at his desk.

"Oh, just so you know," Phaedre whispered in my ear, "all three of your stories were accepted into the literary magazine. Herr Schwarz didn't get a single piece accepted." She reached under her desk and pinched me on the ass.

The rest of the day passed relatively uneventfully. I did pass Thomas Davenport in the hall and he knocked into me, shoving me into a row of lockers. "Pussy," he said under his breath as he passed. It almost made me feel like everything was back to normal again.

At the end of the day I went by Ms. Vasquez's room. She was unpacking a box of books and stacking them on a shelf at the back of the room. I came in and started helping her unpack the books. We didn't speak for several minutes. I stopped for a second and looked at the books we were unpacking. They were copies of *The Exorcist* and *The Joys of Yiddish*.

"You're going to use these books in your class?" I said.

"Yeah."

"You do know that this is a Catholic school, right?"

"It is?" she said. "Jesus, I hope they don't fire me." She handed me a black marker. "Do me a favor. Help me write 'Vasquez' on the side of the pages."

We worked in silence for a few more minutes.

"You know what, Ham?"

"What?"

"You've really got balls," she said, matter-of-factly.

"Thanks," I said.

epilogue

I have decided to add an epilogue to this narrative that I wrote eight years ago.

I spent the whole summer after my freshman year writing down everything that led up to that *apocalyptic*[26] night in May of 1980. I was fourteen when it all happened, which makes me twenty-two now.

When I think back on it now, it seems almost impossible to me that I was really that young. Not that I'm a senior citizen now, but I was just a child then! I see teenagers walking down the street now and they seem like infants to me, so young and small and vulnerable. How could I have lived through those thousand natural shocks (thanks, Hamlet!) and come out whole again on the other side? How do young people do it? I guess a lot of them don't. Some of them prefer to put a stop to all the pain and torture that they can be forced to endure in favor of the peaceful release of death.

The me that I am now is so glad that I never seriously entertained that as an option.

At any rate, a lot of things have happened since then. I wrote most of them down in a journal, and who knows? Maybe I'll publish all of these stories some day for posterity. Although I'm not sure that they would be of any real interest to anyone but me. But maybe I'm selling myself short. Maybe somebody can learn something from all of my experiences. Who knows? At any rate, I thought I should include a couple

---

[26]**a•poc•a•lyp•tic** [*uh*-pok-*uh*-lip-tik] *adj.* 1. resembling an apocalypse 2. forcasting the end of the world 3. relating to the final book of the New Testament, Revelation 4. foretelling of imminent disaster 5. climactic or fundamentally final

How is it possible that a word like this can mean both an end and a beginning?

of the highlights here in my epilogue, and maybe tie this whole emotional story up in a nice tidy bow.

I finished my freshman year at Loyola with very little fanfare. I took my final exams and passed almost all of them with an A (Brother Clive gave me a B+ on my Biology final, I think because I stopped letting him paw me like a horny ape). Dieter Schwarz, Thomas Davenport, Porter Harrison, Amanda Rice, Duane Stemple, Kenneth Lee, and Anton Kovac all graduated that year.

I returned to St. Ignatius Loyola the following year and for that year and each year after that, things got better little by little. Especially since Dieter and Thomas and Porter weren't around. I don't mean to say that people stopped calling me names or knocking my books out of my hands or occasionally tripping me in the cafeteria, but that final half-performance of Hamlet was pretty monumental. A lot of unbelievable things happened after that, but for some reason, that one crazy performance of *Hamlet* didn't seem to bother me as much as it had before. I guess after you live through something as awful as I did, you come out of it a more courageous person. "What doesn't kill me makes me stronger," as my mother always says. I just seemed to be more able to take it all in stride.

The following year I played George Gibbs in the spring production of *Our Town*. I didn't audition my junior year because I was taking too many advanced classes and by the time the spring rolled around I didn't know whether to shit or wind my watch (Ms. Vasquez taught me that expression and I still love it to this day. I highly recommend you use it whenever possible). My senior year I was cast as the lead in *Oedipus Rex* and I brought the house down every night (if I do say so myself).

I took Brother Marvin's Creative Writing class right up until I graduated, and my senior year I was voted the editor-in-chief of the literary magazine. Brother Marvin gave me (on prize day at graduation) a special prize for writing. My mom keeps the trophy on the mantle in the living room.

By the time I reached my senior year I was a captain in the corps and executive officer of B Company. I wore my boots all four years, and I still wear them now even though I never enrolled in ROTC after graduation. They're really comfortable to walk in, and I found out that at college they're actually fashionable. And mine don't even remotely smell of pee.

I graduated in the top ten percent of my class, was a member of the National Honor Society, and earned a partial scholarship to NYU. I was accepted into the Tisch School of the Arts and moved to New York City, where I still live today. Phaedre lives a fifteen-minute ride away on the subway, and we see each other practically every other day.

It's a good thing I read all those books and went to such a good high school and university, because now I can put all of my extensive knowledge to use as I wait tables at night and spend every day going on auditions, 99% of which never lead to anything. But I'm deliriously happy, and I feel pretty certain that something truly great is going to come my way any day now. I can feel it in my bones.

So, "how is this epilogue tying things up in a neat and pretty little bow," you say? Well, two things.

The first thing is that I learned something really important once I got out of high school . . . something that no one ever tells you when you're young and miserable and ready to drink a bottle of Drano®:

High school is like a crucible. A crucible is a container used for heating things to high temperatures. It also means an intense test.

But high school is most certainly not the real world.

And if you can survive that test and move on, there's a good chance that you'll never see any of those people again. You find out very quickly that there are a lot of other people in the world. And some of those people are just like you. Which means you truly are not alone. And any rotten experience eventually passes and a better experience comes along. You just have to hold on and wait it out.

Knowing this may not make one bit of difference if you're suffering through something right now. It may be the faintest of hopes in a sea of hopelessness. But it's true. I'm living proof.

And maybe the second thing I want to include in this little story will help a little more.

I've been back home to visit quite a bit since I graduated high school. And I've changed a lot since then, too. Both emotionally and physically. I got a lot taller and my mom says that I "grew into my looks" which says to me that I must have been pretty dorky-looking when I was in high school but that I have gotten past that clumsy, awkward phase that is adolescence. In college I started working out and I actually enjoy exercising and lifting weights. And we did a lot of yoga at NYU as part of movement classes.

Who cares, right?

I don't write about all of this to tell everybody that I think I'm a total hunk now, but rather to sort of set the scene . . . to let you know that I'm not the same person I was eight years ago (who is?). It's a kind of important detail to the story that I'm about to tell you. And I want to tell you this story because I think it makes a nice little conclusion to the sea of troubles that came before.

It was Christmastime last year and I had taken a week off from my amazingly rewarding job of serving drinks and announcing specials and smiling at people until my face ached so that I could come home and visit my parents.

I had been home for three days, and even though it was really great to see my mom and dad and Sammy and decorate the tree and drink eggnog and listen to Perry Como records, I was starting to get a little cabin fever. So that night I borrowed my mom's car (a luxury in and of itself because I don't have a car in New York) and took a little trip downtown.

On my way into the downtown area I drove past St. Ignatius Loyola. It was late and the building was completely dark. It stood there like an ogre, clothed in shadows and looming over the street as if it was waiting for me.

I pulled over in front of the school, got out of the car and looked up at the building. It was like some monument in a foreign land, like some place I had read about in a book but had never seen in real life.

I stood there for a few minutes, just looking at the stairs and the façade and wondering if I had really spent four years of my life there. It all seemed like a dream. And not a dream that really stays with you, but one of those dreams that you have trouble remembering all the details about when you wake up. A dream filled with all kinds of crazy events that seemed to make sense when you were dreaming them, but then when you wake up and you think about them they don't connect or make any sense at all.

I got back in the car and kept going toward the downtown area. I was going to go to this club called Valhalla. Phaedre had told me that this new club had opened up in a historic old building downtown that used to be an athletic club and gymnasium. So I was going to go there, have a few cocktails, and spend some time staring at cute guys (a pastime that I still haven't grown out of).

As I drove along the same route that the after-school bus used to take, I saw a familiar old building on my right: Auntie Dick's. It was still there—the building short and square and nondescript; the sign in neon (lit up now for nighttime in garish colors of yellow, red, and pink); the door painted a discreet and speakeasy black.

I parked the car in the lot that was tucked behind the building and walked around to the entrance facing the street. As I stood on the sidewalk the door opened and two men walked out, talking and laughing with each other. The jukebox from inside blasted Madonna singing "Into the Groove." This was mixed with a wave of loud talk and laughter.

"Aw, what the hell," I thought and went inside.

The inside was exactly the same as I remembered it, except there were twenty or thirty people there, standing at the bar or sitting in small groups around the few tables. There were two men playing pool at the table in the back while several others leaned against the walls and watched.

I walked up to the bar and leaned one elbow on it. And who turned around to take my order but good old Chet.

"What can I get you, sunshine," he said with a smile, wiping the bar in front of me with a damp towel. He looked me straight in the eye and of course had no idea who I was.

"I'll have a Harvey Wallbanger," I said.

"You've gotta be shitting me," he said, checking my face to see if I was serious. "I haven't made a Harvey Wallbanger since 1975."

"Never mind," I said. "Just give me a vodka and cranberry."

"Could I see your I.D.?" I took out my wallet and showed it to him. "Thanks," he said, grinning a little sheepishly. "Sorry I have to ask, but you look pretty young."

"No problem," I said. "I would've been insulted if you hadn't."

He turned away from me, chuckling and shaking his head. "Harvey Wallbanger. That's a good one, kid." He quickly and deftly made my drink and passed it over to me. "Dollar well drinks until midnight tonight," he said.

I gave him a ten. "Keep the change," I said.

"Thanks, handsome!" He smiled at me and tipped me a wink.

I turned around and looked over the room again, searching for a spot where I could lean and soak up my surroundings. I spotted a shadowy corner near the jukebox and headed over, weaving my way through the crowd.

I stood leaning against the wall, sipping the drink that Chet had made me. There was so much vodka in it, it made my eyes water. Madonna was replaced by Sheena Easton singing "Sugar Walls." I stood there for several minutes, sipping my drink and looking at the crowd and smiling to myself. Had I really come in here at thirteen and tried to order a beer? And God, I had been so scared. And I actually thought I was walking into some purgatory of sin and sinners when all along it was just a place for people to get a drink and hang out with friends. I shook my head and giggled silently to myself.

"Someone's got a secret," a voice slurred at me from my left. I turned to look at him.

It was Dieter Schwarz.

I almost dropped my drink and barely stopped myself from crying out.

"You wanna share your secret with me, sexy?" He was drunk, and almost unrecognizable. But it was definitely Dieter. It was hard to believe that someone could change so much in such a short amount of time. Although he was only four years older than I was, he already looked like he was forty. His face was bloated and his complexion was red and blotchy. In the light from the jukebox I could see the small burst capillaries in his cheeks and on his nose, the ones that come from excessive and extensive drinking.

He fixed his bleary eyes on me, carefully taking a drag on his cigarette while using his other hand to steady himself on the jukebox. I saw absolutely no glint of recognition in his eyes as he did his best to focus on me.

"Why don't you buy me a drink, baby?" he mumbled. "I'd buy us both one, but Chet's already cut me off. Fucking asshole."

"It looks like you've had enough, don't you think?"

"Oh don't be that way, baby." He dropped his cigarette and leaned toward me, breathing his foul breath into my face. "You're one hot stud, you know that?" he said, putting his arm around my neck. I stepped to my right and pulled his arm off of me.

"It was really nice talking to you," I said, doing my best to keep my face expressionless. "But I have to go now."

He stepped to his left and put his hand on the wall next to my head, blocking my exit.

"Listen, don't be a shit." He said, smiling at me like a shark. "I'm being nice to you. Now why don't you be nice to me?"

For just a second I felt a stab of fear in my stomach. But it was gone as soon as it had come. And all that was left was pity.

"Say," he leaned in toward me, a conspiratorial tone creeping into his voice. "You wanna get out of here? We could go back to my place. I only live about five minutes away." He slid the index finger of his right hand down my cheek, along the side of my neck and down the open front of my shirt. It felt like a snake slithering on me, but I stood as still as a statue.

"I can think of all kinds of things I could do for a beautiful man like you. Whaddaya say? You want me to make you feel good?" He smiled slyly at me and looked at me through his cloudy, half-lidded eyes.

"You don't know who I am, do you?" I said.

He pulled his head back an inch or two, his greasy smile sliding off his face. "I thought you looked familiar," he said finally. It was clear he really had no idea who I was.

I grabbed his head and pulled it towards me, kissing him full on the mouth. "You used to call me Sissykins," I said. It took several seconds for the thought to take hold of his booze soaked brain, but when it did I could see a look of sheer horror spread over his face.

He stood looking at me for several moments, his mouth hanging open and his eyes wide with shock. He opened his mouth several times and then shut it again, completely at a loss for what to say. It seemed as if he had sobered up almost immediately and his eyes focused clearly on me for the first time since our conversation had begun.

He stood swaying slightly and looking me up and down. And then suddenly his mouth pulled down in a grimace of pain and I could see his eyes begin to grow moist with tears.

"I'm sorry," he finally whispered. "I'm just so sorry." Then he began to truly weep, like a child who was being scolded by his father. I couldn't stand to look at his bloated, bawling face for another minute.

I pushed him roughly away from me. I guess I pushed him a little harder than I meant to, or maybe it was just because he was so drunk, but he stumbled back a couple of steps and ran ass-first into the table that was behind him, falling to the ground and scattering the people that had been sitting there.

I stepped forward until I was standing directly over him,

then I placed one foot on his chest, pinning him to the ground. As I looked down at him I saw a thousand expressions flash across his face: shock, shame, hatred, self-pity, and finally fear. The bar had gone completely quiet. Even the jukebox had momentarily and perfectly stopped playing. Our eyes were locked onto one another for a long moment. Then I picked my foot up off of him and took a step back. He lay still on the ground and I could see his eyes gleaming and burning with fury and tears.

"Jesus Christ, Dieter." I said, looking down at him. My voice projected all through the small room. "Get off the floor. You should be ashamed of yourself."

I stepped over him and walked to the exit. As I opened the door I turned and looked back at him. He was still lying on the ground, crying like an infant.

I walked out the door and out into the crisp, cold night.

22100981R00109

Made in the USA
Lexington, KY
11 April 2013